Praise for Ryan Brown's "fast-paced, thrilling, and
terribly funny debut" (*Publishers Weekly*)

PLAY DEAD

"Everything a twenty-first-century zombie novel should be."
—Jonathan Maberry, Bram Stoker Award–winning
author of *The King of Plagues*

"*Friday Night Lights* meets *Dawn of the Dead*. . . . Fast, funny, frightening."
—Brad Thor, #1 *New York Times* bestselling
author of *The Athena Project*

"Exciting and satisfying. Watch this guy! He's going to do great things."
—Joe R. Lansdale, Edgar Award–winning
author of *Devil Red*

"A fantastic thriller, a whole bloody lot of fun!"
—A. J. Jacobs, *New York Times* bestselling
author of *My Life as an Experiment*

"Two cultural obsessions collide head-on. . . . Brown handily mixes
elements of horror, coming-of-age sweetness, and gore-soaked com-
edy into a tale that satisfies the same fascination with sports and
bloodlust that it cleverly and thoughtfully critiques."
—*Publishers Weekly* (starred review)

"An outstanding debut [with] pace, energy, tension, and drive. . . . If
you could inject it, it would be a banned substance."
—Lee Child, #1 *New York Times* bestselling
author of *Killing Floor*

ALSO BY RYAN BROWN

Play Dead

THAWED OUT & FED UP

RYAN BROWN

GALLERY BOOKS

NEW YORK   LONDON   TORONTO   SYDNEY   NEW DELHI

Gallery Books
A Division of Simon & Schuster, Inc.
1230 Avenue of the Americas
New York, NY 10020

First Gallery Books trade paperback edition October 2011

GALLERY BOOKS and colophon are registered trademarks of Simon & Schuster, Inc.

For information about special discounts for bulk purchases, please contact Simon & Schuster Special Sales at 1-866-506-1949 or business@simonandschuster.com.

The Simon & Schuster Speakers Bureau can bring authors to your live event. For more information or to book an event contact the Simon & Schuster Speakers Bureau at 1-866-248-3049 or visit our website at www.simonspeakers.com.

Designed by Renata Di Biase

Manufactured in the United States of America

10 9 8 7 6 5 4 3 2 1

Library of Congress Cataloging-in-Publication Data is available.

ISBN 978-1-4391-7156-1
ISBN 978-1-4391-7162-2 (ebook)

THAWED
OUT &
FED UP

PROLOGUE

It's a bad deal, waking up cold and stiff in the back alley of a pool hall, your skin pruned from rain, your lip dangling slobber, and you can't remember how you got there.

Made even worse when you find blood all over you.

Worse still when you realize the blood ain't yours.

Add to this the fact that your own fillet knife is tucked into the waistband of your Levi's, and you begin to suspect that you might be in a bit of a pickle.

That's how it went the morning all this started.

I'd been back in town only two days, and by the looks of things, I was already steeped in shit.

Good news was that I was in a familiar setting. I'd spent a fair share of time smoking in the narrow alley behind the Rack 'Em Up, so I knew the territory well.

I came off the ground on stiff legs, managed an upright position, and shook some feeling into my arms. Then I closed my eyes, drew a deep breath, and ran through a sort of bodily status check. I had no headache, and my stomach felt all right, which meant that I wasn't hungover yet. Which also meant that I was probably still drunk.

Stepping over strewn trash and cigarette butts, I moved to the pool hall's back door and knocked. A full minute passed before I got a dull groan in response.

"That you, Slow Eddie?" I asked.

Another groan.

Slow Eddie was the owner of the Rack 'Em Up. I figured he'd crashed on one of the snooker tables after closing time again. He usually did that when him and Peg were fighting, which was always.

"It's Sam," I said.

"Who?"

"Sam Bonham, you idiot."

"Sam? You back in town?"

"You're talking to me, ain't ya? Open up, I've got a situation out here."

"I ain't decent!"

"You're never decent."

"Go away!"

Slow Eddie had never been much of a morning person. He also wasn't called Slow Eddie for doing things quick.

"Fine, then," I said. "Just answer me one thing. Did I get into a scrap in there last night?"

"Do what?"

"Did I get sideways of someone last night?"

"You weren't in here last night!"

"Of course I was in there last night," I said. "I'm always in there last night."

"Weren't. Now git!"

"So what you're saying is—"

"Git!"

I did, figuring I wouldn't get much out of Slow Eddie until at least noon, maybe one.

I circled the block in search of my truck but didn't find it, so I walked to the Circle K and bought a pack of Salems. The gal working the counter looked a little taken aback by the blood on my shirt and the knife tucked into my waistband.

"It's okay, honey," I said. "I'm a veterinarian."

I lit my first outside the store, slipped the knife into my boot, and took a seat on the front curb. The cigarette got my brain working, but for the life of me, I couldn't remember a thing from the night before.

Matter of fact, I couldn't remember anything from about midmorning the previous day, when I'd pulled into Floyd's Bottle Shop to pick up some Wild Turkey. I'd also bought a scratch-off lottery ticket there. NO LUCK, the ticket had said. Story of my life. After tossing the ticket I'd opened the bottle, and that was the last thing I could recall.

I stood, crushed out the cigarette, and headed east down San Jacinto.

The town was quiet. The rain had stopped overnight, but thick clouds still hung low in a charcoal gray sky. The smell of grease turned me left on Goliad and led me straight into the Busy Bee Diner.

There were a few patrons scattered about the place, but the breakfast rush hadn't hit yet. I took a seat toward the end of the counter near a glass cabinet full of rotating pies. Pearl had a steaming cup of coffee on the counter before I even hit the stool. She studied me for a time, then her eyes narrowed.

"Sam Bonham, is that really you?"

"Pearl."

"I hardly recognized you. What's it been, a couple months?"

"Six."

"You look like hell."

"Hell should be so lucky."

"What in the world have you been up to?"

I sipped some coffee. "Searching for answers, I figure."

"Hope you found some," Pearl said, fixing me with a stern glare. "Hate to think you walked out on your family for nothin'."

I looked at her.

She popped her Doublemint. "Say, what's that all over your shirt?"

"It's autumn rouge," I said, sipping some more coffee. "I'm repainting the doghouse."

"'I's your wife, I'd have you sleeping in it."

"Make it three eggs, runny," I said. "Hash browns, burnt. White toast, buttered. Side of cheese grits. Side of patty sausage. Half a grapefruit. Might as well add a short stack."

"Crossin' a desert?"

"Soakin' up a rough night."

"What happened?"

"Wish I knew."

She studied me some more. "You trying to grow a beard or what?"

"Why, you like it?"

"Kinda patchy."

I just shrugged. "Can I smoke?"

"Sure, just don't let the door hit your butt on the way out."

I put away the Salems.

Pearl popped her Doublemint again, eared her pencil, and headed into the kitchen. I drank coffee and watched the pies rotate. On the radio in the kitchen, Patsy Cline was singing about falling to pieces. I hadn't fallen to pieces myself yet, but I could see it happening if I didn't sort out this deal with the blood and the fillet knife. Plus, I really needed to know where my truck was.

The knife was definitely mine; that much I did know. Trouble was, I couldn't even remember the last time I'd laid eyes on the thing. I saw no reason why it shouldn't still be in my tackle box at home, by which I mean a home that hadn't been mine for some time.

I guess I should say now that Pearl had spoken true. I did run out on my wife and boy six months back. I can't say I'm proud of it, seeing as they're the only two people in this world I care about. Back in high school when I first started courting Georgia, her mother and daddy used to tell her I was no good. One could say I've spent the better part of the last twenty years living down to their expectations.

Drinking might have had something to do with it. I'm not an alcoholic; I'm just a man who drinks all the time because it helps solve my problems. At least my drinking never made me violent. Distant maybe, but never violent. Not with my family, anyway. Sure, I might hack off a man's ear over a pool hustle, but I never once laid an angry hand on George or Sam Junior. It wasn't in me. I love them both too much for that.

I'm not without my finer points. I can hustle nine-ball with the best of them. I can usually fix whatever's broke, 'cept a heart. I can land a smoke ring on a trophy antler from across the room. And I guess for a drywall man you could do a lot worse.

Finer points I got. It's just character and integrity I lack.

Take for instance the Old Lady Holcomb incident three years back. Old Lady Holcomb lives across from the Sonic over on Travis Street. I was doing the drywall in her kitchen, and she accused me of stealing sixty-three dollars from a Folgers can she keeps above the icebox. I denied it, of course, but she still ran me off without pay and threatened to call the law if I ever came back.

Truth is, I did take that money. Spent eleven dollars of it on whiskey. Put down another fifteen on Salems. Then I took what was left to Slow Eddie's back room and took the poker table for six hundred thirty dollars more. Cheated to win it, too. Then I burned through my winnings on a six-day bender and missed Sam Junior's Thanksgiving pageant because of it.

I recall the Old Lady Holcomb incident only to offer some idea of the man my wife and boy were living with when I ran off in search of answers.

Good thing was, I was back in town now, and determined to set things right on the home front once and for all . . . soon as I got to the bottom of this deal with the bloodstained knife, anyway.

As Pearl delivered my breakfast I got to wondering if maybe I'd gone by the house again last night. Maybe that's where my truck was. It made sense, seeing as I'd bought that bottle of Wild Turkey yesterday. Drinking and house watching had gone hand in hand over the past two days.

I sopped up some egg yolk with a corner of white toast and let my eyes drift back to the pies, turning in circles, going nowhere fast. I related.

Minutes later, two men appeared at the counter on either

side of me. In the reflection of the milk locker, I could see that they were cops. They smelled like rain and menthol snuff. The man on my left set down a Stetson wrapped in a plastic rain cover and ran his fingers through wet hair.

Pearl came over and both men ordered coffee.

"You boys look like hell," Pearl said, her favorite greeting.

"Tough morning," said the cop on my right. "Better make them coffees to go, Pearl. We're on the clock."

"Into overtime now, aren't you?"

The cops shared a look over my head.

"Whole damn force'll be pulling OT on this one, I reckon."

"On what?"

"Had ourselves a homicide in town last night, sugar."

Coffee dribbled onto the countertop as Pearl looked up. "Did I just hear you right?" she asked.

The cop on my right gave a solemn nod. "Got us a bloody damn mess of a dead man sprawled across this young gal's front lawn over on Shady Glen Road."

My fork clattered to the plate.

"Don't that beat all?" asked the cop on my left. "A fatal stabbing right here in Welshland, Texas." He made a rueful click with his cheek. "Good-lookin' young man, too. Such a waste."

"Well, who was he?" Pearl asked.

"He carried no ID, but they're runnin' plates now. Don't think he's a local."

"Worst part is," said the other cop, "it was the woman's boy found the body. Poor kid's probably damaged for life." He shook his head. "Never in my twenty-one years on the force . . ."

There was a thoughtful pause between the three of them.

I subtly tugged my ball cap down low over my eyes.

"Anyway, we best get on back," said the cop on my left. "Chief's got some hard-core boys from County comin' in to do lab work. Them County boys ain't gonna mess around on this deal, I'll tell you that."

"That ain't no lie," agreed his partner.

"Real sorry to upset you with this, Pearl."

Pearl asked if they had any leads on who might have done it.

The cop on my right shook his head. "But don't you worry, honey . . ." He took a toothpick off the counter and set it between clenched teeth. "There ain't a badge in this county gonna sleep till the sumbitch is slow roastin' in hell."

He winked at Pearl, then placed some money on the counter. Pearl told him not to be silly, and he put it away. She asked the men if they wanted some biscuits to go.

The cops declined, thanked her kindly, tipped their hats, and moved off.

I quickly folded my arms over my bloody shirt.

Me and Pearl shared a look.

She shook her head slowly. "You think you know a town and the people in it . . ."

I told her I couldn't believe it, either.

Trouble was, I could.

As it happened, my wife and boy lived on Shady Glen Road.

1.

I sobered up quick then, waiting desperately for Pearl to move off so I could get hell and gone from there before she considered the cops' story and my red-stained shirt and put two and two together. Didn't help that Pearl picked that moment to get back to her crossword puzzle just a few feet down the counter from me.

Torturous minutes passed. My mind began to reel, recalling what all had transpired in the past thirty-six hours . . . or at least those parts I could remember.

I went back to the moment I'd returned to town the night before last. It had been well after dark. Minus the odd stop for gas and food, I'd been driving for more than fourteen hours and had gone long past road weary.

After grabbing a drive-through Dairy Queen burger and a bottle of Wild Turkey at Floyd's, I'd decided to post up somewhere for the night and plan my next move. When you've run out on your family for a stretch of months, leaving them with no idea where you went to, it can be a tricky deal crawling back to ask forgiveness. I figured if I was going to pass the night in my truck, thinking and planning, I might as well do it in a familiar setting.

I parked some seventy-five yards down the street from the house on Shady Glen, just past the bend in the road. The spot offered a good view of the house but was far enough away not to draw suspicion. Good thing was, I was driving a truck that no one would recognize. My old truck had given out weeks back. The new one I'd won in a card game back in Pewly Flats.

Staring at the place through the bug-stained windshield for hour upon hour, I had plenty opportunity to take in every detail of the house and yard. The dogwood I planted the day we moved in. The sun-cracked garden hose I'd been meaning to replace, but hadn't. The waterlogged Nerf ball Sam Junior always leaves on top of the holly bush just off the porch. I took some comfort in seeing that not much had changed in my absence.

It was near midnight when I first caught sight of George's silhouette moving past the living room drapes. After sixteen years of marriage I could make a pretty good guess that she was heading to the kitchen for Lucky Charms. George always ate cereal when she got hungry at night. I couldn't make out any details in the silhouette, but I figured she'd be in one of her tank-top-and-shorts combos that she sleeps in. Just the mental image of it was enough to get the old flame burning again.

My wife, George, has the kind of looks that could inspire epic poetry. Red hair. Green eyes. Freckles between her bosoms. Skin that looks tan even in the winter. Her shape hasn't changed a lick since her days on the high school drill team, either.

I took a healthy belt of Wild Turkey, hoping it might douse my arousal, but it proved to have the opposite effect. By the time George's silhouette moved past the window again, I'd been worked into quite a lather. My hand went for the door handle. It was all I could do not to jump out of the truck right then, go ring the bell, and get started on setting things right.

But I resisted.

I hadn't thought it all through yet. A situation like this has to be handled just right, I knew, and I needed a plan.

I took another drink. Then another.

A plan never came. But sleep soon did.

I don't know what time I awoke in the morning, but the sun was out and the morning dew was beaded up on the windshield. I rose stiffly on the bench seat and popped my neck and back. My head throbbed. My mouth tasted sour. My eyes were caked with crud.

The bottle lying in the floorboard was empty.

I pulled a Salem from the box on the dash, got lit, and flipped the wiper switch to clear the dew off the glass.

No sooner had I done it than movement caught my eye—Sam Junior bounding out of the garage on the side of the house. He was riding a bike I didn't know he had. First thing I noticed was how big he'd gotten, looking every bit of his twelve years and then some. He was still scrawny, but there was some shape to him now. His limbs had stretched, and his shoulders had taken some form. He wasn't just knobby knees and elbows anymore.

Second thing I noticed was how good he rode that bike. Ball cap turned backward, hair blown back; he was hopping curbs and riding wheelies like him and the bike were a part of the same well-oiled machine.

I slumped low in the seat and watched him do a few turns

and work some tricks. Once, he passed no more than twenty feet in front of the truck, and I had to duck so as not to be seen.

For some time the boy put on quite a show, until he came up short trying to curb jump the fireplug next to the driveway. The cigarette fell from my lips as I watched him sail over the handlebars. I was out of the car and running at full stride by the time his head hit the ground.

He'd been lucky. Four more inches and his skull would have hit concrete instead of grass. By the time I'd hustled up behind him, he was already sitting upright and shaking grass out of his hair.

"You all right?"

"I'm cool," he said.

He stood on unsteady legs. I saw that his top lip was already swollen. There was also a bruise above his left elbow.

"Should ice that lip," I said.

"Huh?" Dazed, the boy dabbed the lip with his finger. "No, that . . . that happened yesterday."

I could tell he was still rattled by the fall, if not a little embarrassed. He kept his body turned as he dusted himself off.

"We should get you some protective gear," I said. "You nearly gave me a heart attack, Sam."

He stopped, turned, and looked up. "Do I know you, mister?"

"Mister, hell . . . it's me!"

His eyes blinked. "Dad?"

"Hell, yes, Dad, who'd you think it was?"

"I just wasn't expecting . . . I mean . . . well, what's with that beard?"

"You like it?"

The boy thought about it. "Kinda patchy." He looked me up and down. His manner suddenly became guarded, like he wasn't sure how he was supposed to react. "What are you doing here?"

Behind us, the front door of the house swung open. George stepped out, fumbling to tie her bathrobe over her tank top and short-shorts. She was barefoot. Her legs looked tan and silky.

"Sam!" she hollered.

"Yeah?" The boy and I replied in unison.

Georgia came marching down the walk.

"Hi, honey," I said, smiling. "That bacon I smell in there?"

I never saw the punch coming. She hit me in the nose, hard enough to well tears.

"Mom! That's Dad you just socked!"

Georgia told Sam Junior to get back in the house this instant.

Sam Junior stayed where he was.

I wiped my eyes with my sleeve and looked back at my wife. "Now I can see how you might be pissed—"

"I'd still have to care to be pissed," she said. "I'm long past that. That punch was just fulfilling a promise I made to myself months ago."

Her voice was calm. Calmer than I would have liked. I'd have much preferred anger to quiet resolve.

"Can I come in?" I said.

"No."

"If you'll just hear me out—"

The man said nothing. He pulled a Marlboro out of his shirt pocket and put a flame to it. Smoke trickled through his thin smile.

Georgia folded her arms across her chest. Her eyes fell to the ground.

I approached her up the walk. "Don't do this," I said.

"It's done, friend," the man said. "You best be getting on now."

I cut my eyes over to him. "I ain't your friend. And no one tells me to get off my own damn lawn."

Sam Junior started to say something, but the man stepped forward, closing the distance between us, and Sam Junior held his tongue.

"We're not gonna have trouble here, are we?" the man asked.

His tone was level, but I noticed a fist coiling at his side.

I had to crane my neck to look him in the eye.

Georgia answered his question before I could.

"There's not gonna be any trouble, Slick," she said. "Sam was just leaving."

I looked at her. "George, you gotta believe me now. I've changed. Just give me the chance to show you."

"It's too late," she said.

"It ain't," I said. "You just gotta take a leap and trust me." I raised her chin with my finger. "I leaped a cliff for you once upon a time, didn't I? All I ask is that you do the same for me now."

The man moved my finger off of George's chin.

I jerked my hand away and drew it back, ready to swing.

"Don't . . ." The man's voice was deep. His cigarette still hung limp between his lips. "That'd be a big mistake, I can promise you."

Now the man had both fists coiled. His breathing was still slow and steady.

"He's right, Dad," said Sam Junior. "Get on outta here now. It's best for everyone." I looked at the boy. He looked back at me. "You should know there are no more doors need fixing in this house, anyway."

The man tipped his Stetson to me. He turned Georgia and Sam around and led them both up the walk. I went back to my truck, gunned the motor, and drove like hell. Minutes later I was in Floyd's parking lot, cracking the seal on that bottle of Wild Turkey.

That was yesterday morning, and that was still the last thing I could remember before waking up in the alley behind the Rack 'Em Up.

A bell dinged. I looked up to see Pearl set her pencil down on her crossword puzzle and retreat into the kitchen at last. I tossed a few wrinkled bills onto my plate and hustled outside. Two minutes later I was speeding through town in a hot-wired Buick, taken from the Whataburger parking lot across the street from the diner.

I didn't stop until I reached Charon's Bridge, which crossed the Trebok River on Welshland's north side. I parked in the center of the bridge and barely made it out of the car in time to chuck what little I'd eaten over the bridge rail. I sent the fillet knife into the river right behind it.

The world seemed to be spinning around me. My limbs felt numb. My breath was short. Thinking I might faint, I planted my elbows on the rail, lowered my head, and took a few deep breaths.

My head was filled with too many thoughts to process at

once. I just couldn't believe that I had it in me to do such a thing. No doubt the square-jawed cowboy had pissed me off something fierce, stepping up to me like he had, belittling me in front of my boy, taking all that was mine for his ownself. But Christ, could I have really been pissed enough to go back and gut the son of a bitch in a blind drunk?

A siren wailed in the distance, and my body went rigid.

I looked at the stolen Buick parked behind me, door open, engine running.

I scanned the length of the bridge in both directions.

One way led east, back toward Welshland, from where there were now two sirens screaming.

The other way led west toward . . . everywhere else.

West it was.

2.

I hit Waxahachie by midmorning and ditched the Buick there, switching it out for a late-model Ford pickup. From Waxahachie, I veered southwest, just following my nose, keeping to the back roads, not yet thinking about a destination. My mind was still swimming. The towns flew by as quick as the Salems burned.

I hit Lampasas at noon and Pontotoc around one. The pedal stayed floored until midafternoon, when hunger and fatigue finally led me into the Lasso Burger just outside Menard.

There I added another crime to my rap sheet, realizing only after I'd scarfed a shrimp-and-rib combo that I'd dropped my last dollar in my hurried exit from the Busy Bee. I'd had no choice but to walk the check, but managed to get clear of the town without incident.

No question something had to get done about the cash situation.

Also there was the issue of my bloody shirt, which had become as itchy as it was unsightly. I pressed on for a couple more hours, but finally stopped in Thedford, a depressing little one-stoplight town you wouldn't find on most maps.

Creeping down Thedford's only drag, I came across the Bluebonnet Variety Store and headed in to see about getting some new clothes.

The store was bigger inside than it looked outside, and I was surprised to find a handful of shoppers milling up and down the narrow aisles. I wasted no time snatching a purse from the shopping cart of a distracted old woman studying a rack of panty hose. She had no wallet or credit cards, but carried sixty-seven dollars in cash—plenty for a pair of Wranglers, a pearl-snap shirt, some nice tube socks, a three-pack of underwear, and some Juicy Fruit.

From there I headed to the coin-op car wash at the end of the street and hosed myself down, standing buck naked in the open door of the pickup. I threw on my new clothes and was eager to keep moving, but decided first to spend my remaining six dollars on gas before pressing on.

The Gas 'N Snack was a half mile outside the western edge of town. A tall neon sign above the roof read LAST STOP FOR GAS. It didn't say till when.

The station was a pay-before-you-pump outfit. On my way into the store I passed a pay phone and wondered if it might be worth risking a quick call to the Rack 'Em Up to see what I could learn about the situation back home. The phone rang a good twenty times before Slow Eddie answered with a belch.

"It's Sam," I said.

"Who?"

"It's Sam Bonham, you idiot."

"Sam? Kee-rist, are you in a pickle."

"Pickle?"

"Someone's been kilt outside your wife's place."

"Who got killed?"

"Real good-looking fella from what I hear. Tall, too."

"Slow Eddie, listen, I don't have much—"

"Sam, you should know the cops came in here earlier to ask if you were . . . hold on . . ."

The line went silent.

"Hello?" I said. "Slow Eddie, you there? Listen, if the cops are there with you right now and you can't talk to me, just say Elmer Fudd."

A full minute passed.

I started to get anxious.

Then finally, "What the fuck's Elmer Fudd got to do with any of this, Sam?"

"Damnit, Slow Eddie, put Elwood on!"

Elwood Turner and I had run a few pool hustles together over the years. He didn't have any more sense than Slow Eddie, but he usually did things faster.

"He's smoking out back," Slow Eddie said.

"Put him on!"

Four minutes later, Elwood came on.

"Sam?"

"Yeah, it's me. Listen, I don't have much—"

"When'd ya get back in town, you old butthole?"

"That's not important," I said. "I need you to tell me what you—"

"You know, I ought not be talking to you, Sam. You're hot, and I'm on parole."

"I'm hot?"

"People say you murdered him."

"Which people? Murdered who?"

"Cops. They say you killed a fella by the name of Slick Motley. Where are you anyway?"

"Des Moines."

"The fuck you doing in Ohio?"

"Skip it. What else can you tell me about this killing?"

"You want the good news or the bad?"

"Give me the good."

"There ain't none."

"Give me the bad."

"Bad news is, the cops found a truck with your prints all over it parked down the street from Georgia's house this morning. They found footprints in her yard that match the make of your Tony Lama's. Last night one of Georgia's neighbors overheard a confrontation in your old lady's front yard, and claims one of the voices was yours. Your fingerprints were found on the stiff's wristwatch and belt buckle. Some waitress at the Busy Bee claims you came by this morning with blood splattered all over your shirtfront. There's reports that you stole a cripple lady's Buick and skipped town. The old lady has since fallen because you drove off with her walker in the trunk. Word is her hip's gone outta whack and her health care's for shit."

I agreed that this was bad news.

"Also, Slow Eddie says your beer tab's past due."

"How you getting your information, Elwood?"

"Chet Lindo."

"Who's Chet Lindo?"

"Guy I'm shootin' pool with. He's pluggin' Tina Tillwell."

"Who's Tina Tillwell?"

"She works the dispatch desk at the Welshland PD. Tina tells Chet about everything comin' and goin' over at that station house. Just a sec . . ."

I heard chalk squeak, then the clack of pool balls.

"Sorry, Sam, had to sink the seven."

"Anything else you can tell me, Elwood?"

"I don't guess."

"You sure?"

"Well, there is one thing. They've launched a statewide manhunt for you."

"Who's they?"

"A multijurisdictional task force, or some damn thing. Fella named Turkey Shoot Johnson's been put in charge of the op."

"I'm an op?"

"T. S. Johnson don't play around, from what I hear. Big bastard. Crack shot. 'Nam vet, and all that."

"Anything else for me?"

"Just a question, Sam."

"Go ahead."

"When you get the chair, can I have your truck?"

I hung up and headed into the store.

I tried the men's room door but found it locked, so I went on up to the register.

The kid working the counter was maybe nineteen, with spiky hair, wire braces, and acne. But he looked friendly enough.

Too friendly, it seemed, after a moment's consideration. Something about the kid's smile wasn't quite ringing true.

"How's your day goin'?" he asked through a wide grin.

"Why do you ask?" I narrowed my eyes.

The kid frowned. "Just being friendly, is all."

I held his stare for a few beats but saw nothing suspicious behind his eyes.

It occurred to me that my talk with Elwood Turner had already left me paranoid.

"John's locked," I said.

"Key's in the back," he said. A phone rang. The kid smiled and jabbed a thumb over his shoulder. "Phone's back there, too. I'll just be a sec."

He moved into the back.

I dropped a five and a single onto the counter for the gas and tried to shake the paranoid feeling that had come over me. It wouldn't shake. I looked out the storefront window and imagined that Turkey Shoot Johnson and his boys were already on me, standing behind the bushes across the street, riflescopes on my head, just waiting for me to step outside so they wouldn't have to splatter the candy shelf with my brains and hair.

It wasn't a pleasant thought.

I tried to laugh it off and chalk it up to Elwood's dumb ass playing tricks with my head. Trouble was, the more my thoughts went in that direction, the further my imagination took them. Just how close could those lawmen be? I'd ditched the Buick back in Waxahachie almost six hours ago. Surely they'd found it by now. Surely by now the pickup I'd replaced it with had been reported, too. And wouldn't someone have called in that check I walked back at the Lasso Burger outside Menard?

Who's to say a team of lawmen hadn't been holed up somewhere since early this morning playing connect the dots across a Texas road map, following me every step of the way and closing in fast? Christ, what about the purse I'd snatched at the Bluebonnet Variety some twenty minutes ago, just a half mile up the street? If it had been reported, someone might have checked a store camera and seen . . .

Camera.

My eyes drifted up, and there it was, right under the Schlitz sign, pointed right at me.

Movement drew my focus into the back room. The kid was still on the phone. I probably wouldn't have given it a second thought had he not cupped a hand over his mouth. He glanced back at me, and I saw fear in his eyes that hadn't been there before.

I cut my gaze back to the window just as an SUV appeared over the rise about a quarter mile up the road, coming from the direction of town. The vehicle had a light bar above the roof. It was approaching fast.

A cold sweat broke over me.

The boy still had the phone pressed to his ear. I heard him say a few "yes, sir"s and "I understand"s under his breath.

He'd gone pale, even though I suspected he was being told to remain calm and act natural. I looked at my truck parked out by the pump, then again at the SUV. I'd never make it to the truck.

I backed away from the counter and looked down the short hallway that led to the back of the store. There was a rear exit door at the end of the hall, just past the bathroom.

I started toward it, but stopped when an idea struck. I moved back into the main room.

"Hey, kid . . ." I said. "Better hurry along with that key. I got some chili coming back on me quick."

The kid looked unsure how to respond. The phone receiver was still pressed to his ear. He finally tossed me the key.

"Mind if I borrow a *Field and Stream?*" I asked, grabbing the latest issue off the magazine rack. "Figure to be in there a spell."

The kid mumbled some response, and I retreated into the hallway.

I tossed the magazine and the key onto the men's room floor, hit the lock button on the knob, then stepped out and slammed the door closed, loud enough for the kid to take note of it. I then tiptoed to the rear door, slid the lock, and stepped outside without a sound.

I moved to the edge of the building and peered around the corner just as the SUV swerved onto the property. There was another police car now, approaching only seconds behind the SUV. I saw the kid run outside to meet the vehicles. Two lawmen in felt Stetsons stepped out of the SUV, hands on their sidearms. The kid moved between them, gesturing wildly and pointing back toward the store.

The squad car pulled onto the lot and two more men stepped out, both carrying shotguns. Once I saw them moving toward the store, I took off.

The gas station backed up to a weedy, littered field that extended about fifty yards before dropping off sharply into what looked like a creek bed. Beyond that was woods.

I covered a good thirty yards across the field before risking a look back.

The store's rear door was still closed.

I kept going and didn't slow pace until I reached the edge of the drop. At the bottom of the grade, some sixty feet below, a narrow creek trickled over a bed of rocks and weeds.

I paused only long enough to set my feet, then jumped.

The instant I went airborne, the gas station's rear door clanged open.

I was tumbling in a barrel roll by the time I hit the creek bed. I got to my feet quick, high-stepped through the shallow water, then continued on into the trees.

Some fifteen seconds later I heard a car engine roar to life back at the gas station.

A siren screamed.

I kept moving, hopping rocks and weaving through trees, dry limbs whipping my face and arms.

I must have gone at least a mile before the woods thinned out, putting me back into the open. Beyond the tree line the ground sloped upward for about twenty yards. When I topped the rise, I was on a two-lane country road.

I staggered into the middle of the road, wheezing, barely able to draw breath. I'd lost all sense of direction. Sirens were still screaming somewhere in the distance.

A car appeared up the road, and I immediately made a move back toward the trees. But on another glance, I realized that it was a civilian car, an old Plymouth.

I smoothed down my hair and drew a few deep breaths to regain composure.

The car began to brake as soon as my hand went up. The driver was alone. He pulled up beside me and leaned across the front seat to roll down the passenger's-side window.

"Hi-dee," he said. "Help ye?"

He was country folk, old and skinny and missing some teeth.

"Hope you can," I said.

"What's the trouble?"

"Damndest thing . . ." I opened the passenger door and got in the car. "Last night on a bender I hacked up my wife's boyfriend with a fillet knife and left him for dead on her front lawn. Now I need your car."

Twenty seconds later the old man was a speck in my rear-view mirror; the Plymouth's speedometer needle was pegged at one twenty, and before me was nothing but a white dotted line stretching to the horizon.

3.

My eyes stayed glued to the rearview mirror for a good while, checking for flashing lights. More than an hour passed before I even started to relax.

In that time I might have passed a handful of cars at the most, but none of them were marked. The terrain changed a lot in the first hundred miles outside Thedford. I'd left woodlands behind and come into open plain country, where anything taller than a scrub brush was a rare sight.

Preoccupied as I'd been with checking my tail, I hadn't even considered my destination. It was only when the late-afternoon sun broke through the passenger's-side window that it occurred to me I was headed due south.

And that's when it hit me.

I'd keep on heading south.

To Mexico.

Wasn't that where fleeing murderers were supposed to go? Weren't there little towns down there just crawling with outlaw gringos like myself, burning up their years under the sun, a tattered sombrero sitting crooked on their heads, a pickled worm floating at the bottom of the bottle in their fist?

In truth, the picture didn't particularly appeal to me. But then, neither did sixty to life in Huntsville. Or the chair. Or a skull plugging from Turkey Shoot Johnson's assault rifle.

Mexico . . .

The prospect seemed as daunting as it was promising. How the hell would I manage? The only Mexican I spoke were cuss words I'd picked up at the Rack 'Em Up. Could I get the Plymouth across the border, or would I have to swim? Where would I sleep? What would I eat? How would I pay for it?

I had no answers.

But I kept going, boot pressed firm to the pedal, teeth gnashing hard on Juicy Fruit.

It was like fate had taken the wheel, and I guess I found a little comfort in that.

For a short while, anyway.

Until fate bit me in the ass.

4.

One thing about Texas—it's goddamn big.

I'm told you could fit about six Arizonas in it, and still have room left over for the odd Delaware.

Still, you never really get a sense of just how big it is until you've spent eleven hours driving across it without hitting a state line.

Or until you get stranded in it on a desolate stretch of road.

The sign above the Gas 'N Snack in Thedford had read true; it did prove to be the last stop for gas.

I'd been pressing the Plymouth hard for more than three hours when the tank finally went dry and the vehicle sputtered to a jarring halt. After a lengthy bout of cussing and dashboard pounding, I caught a look at myself in the rearview mirror and hardly recognized the wild-eyed visage looking back at me. My coal black hair, normally pomade-slick and swept straight back, had gone curly and wild. My bloodshot eyes had sunk deep. My face, somewhat angular by nature, looked even more withered and drawn than usual.

I reached into my shirt pocket for a Salem and cussed some more when I realized I'd smoked my last just outside

Thedford. I drew a few breaths to clear my head. One thing was certain: if the law was still on my tail, I was a sitting duck. My escape from the Gas 'N Snack had been narrow, and more than a little lucky. And while it appeared that I'd been in the clear for the past couple hours, there was no reason to think those lawmen weren't still in chase and closing in fast.

I figured the best I could do was hitch—or hijack—another ride, but I hadn't seen so much as a power line in the past forty minutes, much less another car coming or going.

I scanned the horizon. Daylight was fading fast. The sunset had dust in it, the way Texas sunsets usually do. A rusty shade of orange had wiped all the blue out of the sky.

Time passed. The sky grew darker.

Then there was movement in the rearview mirror. Headlights. But I couldn't tell if it was a squad car or civilian.

I got out of the Plymouth and, keeping low, sprinted off the road some hundred and fifty yards, until I reached a clutch of scrub brush tall enough to hunker behind.

Minutes later the car crept up behind the Plymouth. It was a squad car. Two men in Stetsons got out. Flashlight beams passed over my head, sweeping the area. I could faintly hear the squawk of a police radio. I kept myself pressed low to the ground.

Soon another set of headlights appeared—an unmarked SUV. Three more men with flashlights stepped out.

My mouth had gone dry. My heart rate picked up.

I looked around. Night had fallen completely. The moon was hidden behind cloud, and the land was dark.

I figured my choice was to run like hell or wait the men out, at the risk that they might decide to spread out and search the area on foot.

I'd never been very good at waiting.

I don't how far I'd traipsed through the darkness before my legs finally gave out, but it had been miles. I'd been so tired, I couldn't even remember collapsing to the dirt to fall asleep.

When I awoke it was daylight, and a steady sprinkle of rain was falling from a low ceiling of cloud. The temperature had dropped enough for me to see my breath. With movement being the only way to warm myself, I stood, stretched, pissed, and pressed on.

By midmorning the sprinkles had turned to heavy showers. By noon I was walking through an outright storm. The wind kicked up. Thunder cracked, and lightning shot in clawlike streaks. Every raindrop seemed to hit me like a pinprick.

The terrain scarcely changed. There was flat nothingness in all directions. My feet grew raw, and my body shook from the cold. Still, I kept moving, and the hours ticked by.

As there was no sun to set, night just sort of fell. I wandered through the stormy darkness for more than an hour before shelter finally revealed itself to me in an extended flash of lightning. It was a small overhang, cut into the side of a gully beside a fast-running stream, which I figured had been a dry riverbed only hours before.

I moved to it quick and climbed inside. I sat with my knees huddled under my chin and watched the water rush by. When

I couldn't fight off sleep any longer, I tumped onto my side, curled into a ball, and shut my eyes.

The dream came on quick.

It was summer, and I was thirteen.

I was tan and shirtless and walking confident in new Levi's and old boots, which lent me a couple extra inches under the heel.

I stepped out of our screen door and found Mama on the front porch, drinking sweet tea and smoking a Merit in her favorite yellow dress. It was before the sickness came. She looked young and healthy.

She also looked troubled.

She hugged me and asked where I was off to.

I just told her I was off.

She told me to be sweet and to be careful and to treat the ladies nice.

I asked her which ladies, and she told me *every* lady. It's important for a man to treat a lady nice, she said.

Like Daddy treats you, I said.

Tears welled in her eyes, and I asked her what was the matter.

She told me I was starting to look like Daddy.

I smiled and headed down the walk. I stepped out into the street, and when I looked back Mama had turned away and her shoulders were shaking like she was crying.

The dreamed changed then, suddenly, like a channel had been switched.

I was older now, sixteen, and more filled out.

I was in cutoffs, a T-shirt, and one of Daddy's bent-up cowboy hats with a sweat stain around the brim.

Standing before me was Georgia. She was sixteen, too.

We stood in a wide-open field, waist deep in weeds.

She wore a pink summer dress that she almost filled out. She was barefoot, with chipped toe polish. Her skin was sunkissed and freckled, her long red hair wind-blown. Lip gloss shined on her mouth. Her perfume smelled like candy.

I took off Daddy's hat and held it in a fist at my waist.

I told Georgia it was nice to make her acquaintance. I told her she'd caught my eye while carrying the Lone Star in the color guard before the football games.

She told me she'd noticed me playing flanker, and liked how I kept low to the ground when I ran the ball.

I thanked her.

She told me she liked the smell of my hair pomade.

I told her it was coconut flavor. I asked if maybe she wanted to do something.

She said like what.

Like drink Dr Pepper. Maybe smoke some cigarettes.

She just laughed and turned away. She took off running across the field like she wanted me to chase her.

I did.

Her tan legs moved quick. Her summer dress clung and fluttered in all the right places. She kept running and I kept chasing, and we both kept laughing.

Just as I thought the field would go on forever, she leaped and disappeared off the cliff at the edge of the ravine.

I started to leap in after her, but stopped at the edge instead.

I watched her break the surface of the river far below.

She looked up, laughing, her hand shielding her eyes from the sun.

She told me to jump, but I didn't. I just kept looking at her. Her hair was swept straight back. When she smiled, her wire braces caught the sunlight.

Jump, she said.

Not yet, I answered.

You're teasin' me, she said. Didn't your mama tell you it ain't nice to tease a girl?

I told her that Mama was sick. I told her that Mama was dying.

She said she was sorry and hadn't meant nothing by it.

I told her I knew that.

Her smile came back.

The straps of her summer dress had fallen off her shoulders, and I wondered if it was on purpose.

She told me again to jump.

She called me chicken and laughed.

I laughed with her but still I hesitated, taking in the sight of her, wanting the moment to stretch.

I decided then that she was the one.

She'd always be the one.

I took a step back, then leaped.

I hate dreams.

Always have.

Whether good or bad, they always play tricks. Cruel damn tricks. Especially when they replay scenes from your past just as they really happened.

At first I thought it was thunder that had yanked me out of the dream.

The loud boom had launched me off the cold shale so fast that I bumped my head on the overhang. Swimming dots filled my vision. I shook my head to clear them and peered outside.

In the distance I saw a huge white flickering light, which was undoubtedly some kind of fire. My first thought was lightning, but then I wondered what lightning could have hit that would burn. The storm was still raging as strong as ever. The rain hadn't let up a bit.

The rushing stream before me had become more like a raging river in the time I'd been asleep. It had also risen a good bit, coming almost level with me. The thought of leaving the shelter and crossing the river didn't appeal, but the thought of getting close to fire did. I studied the water for a time. It didn't look deep, maybe six feet at the most, but that would still put it seven inches over my head. And I figured it to be a good sixty feet across.

Knowing that the flames wouldn't last long in the storm, I wondered if a few minutes of warmth was worth the risk of drowning. The chatter of my teeth and the numbness in my fingers told me that it was.

I came up to a crouch, took a moment to muster my courage, took a deep breath, then tumped headlong into the foam.

Turned out I couldn't have reached the bottom no matter how shallow the water was; it was moving too fast to get my legs underneath me. My boots slammed into rocks and got tangled on weeds. A couple times I went under, only to resurface coughing up water. Panic kept my limbs churning, and soon I was closing in on the opposite bank. Surrendering to

walk down the rest of the slope. The town was another quarter mile from the base of the plateau.

I circled a wide berth in my approach so as to come in on the town's east end, near the water tower. A sign built of scrap lumber stretched across the road about twenty feet off the ground. It read BLISTERED VALLEY in flaking red letters that looked like a child might have painted them. I was fixing to head under it when a man stepped out from the shade of the tower.

"The hell you think you're going, shorty?"

He was a cowboy. Not the sort of yokel you'd find at a Garth Brooks concert, but a real cowboy. He was tall, maybe six feet, unshaven, and scraggly. His clothes were dust-caked. The front brim of his hat was curled back like the lid of a sardine can. I put him at about my age, but he had the wear and tear of a man much older. There was sand trapped in the creases of his face. He had a nose that had been broken more than once.

He also had a six-gun holstered at each hip, which was why, for the moment, I decided to let the "shorty" slide.

"Howdy there, partner," I said, keeping things light. "Dressed early for the square dance?"

The cowboy drew both guns and aimed one at my head and the other at my balls.

My hands went up.

"How'd you get here?" he asked.

"That's a long story."

"Anyone know you're here?"

"I sure hope not."

"We don't want your kind."

"What kind's that?"

"Anyone ain't already in. It's law."

"Whose law?"

"Red Danyon. My brother."

"What say you go get your brother then, have him tell me that his ownself?"

"Red won't be as polite as me. He'd have shot your short ass already."

Again with the short talk. It was starting to rankle me.

I heard a tinny piano playing in the distance and took a step sideways to look beyond the cowboy. The street behind him was still empty. Under the music I heard the faint sound of clinking glasses.

I shifted back in front of the man. "Look, Slim, I don't want any trouble. Passing through is all I'm doing. I get a good square meal and a sip or two of something hard, and I'll be on my way."

The cowboy told me to go back the way I came.

I told him to kiss my ass.

Leather creaked as he stepped toe-to-toe with me. One of his pistols came up and pressed hard against my left nostril. The other gun went down the waistband of my jeans. His breath stank of last night's whiskey.

I peered upward to meet his eyes. I felt no fear. Maybe it was the thirst, hunger, and fatigue. Maybe it was because this wasn't the first time I'd had to face down a bully cutting short jokes. Whichever the case, I was more pissed off than scared.

"Friend, you don't want to do this," I said.

His lips parted to show me his tooth. "Why's 'at?"

"'Cause I no longer trust myself in moments of confrontation."

His smile grew wide. His eyes narrowed. "Where you from, stranger?"

I jabbed a thumb over my shoulder.

"Where you headed?"

I pointed over his shoulder.

We held gazes for a few beats. His guns pressed harder against their targets.

He shook his head. "I don't think so . . ."

My hands moved like lightning as he pulled both triggers.

There were two dull clicks as metal clamped down on skin. I felt the hard squeeze of the gun hammers on each of my thumbs, but registered no pain from it.

Our eyes held.

There was shock on the cowboy's face. His jaw dropped low enough for a rope of spit to fall.

"How did you—"

"I'm fast, that's how."

"No one's that fast."

My forehead ramming into his chin proved otherwise. He tumbled backward a few steps before his ass hit the dirt.

I freed the guns from my hands and tossed them away, then stepped forward and took in my first dusty breath of Blistered Valley. The place even tasted soulless.

I took the cowboy by the collar and dragged him back into the shadows beneath the water tower. Wooden barrels were stacked all around. I leaned the cowboy up against one of them, knelt in front of him, and yanked up a fistful of his hair so that I was sure I had his attention.

"I don't intend on any more problems with you, hoss. In my wake is a dead man with a chest full of knife wounds and an old lady with a bum hip and no walker . . . both because of me. I trust you'll remember that."

He started to speak, but I shoved his head against the barrel, quick and hard, knocking him cold before he got a word out.

His hat caught the wind and blew up against my leg.

I put it on, cocked it to the right, and found it to be a good fit. I bent the front brim down low over my eyes and felt satisfied.

There was a humming sound to my left. Crouched low behind one of the barrels was a young dark-skinned boy, his big brown eyes peering at me over the harmonica wedged between his lips. He blew another quiet note.

I tipped my hat to him, then headed up the street in search of the source of the clinking glasses.

"The other cowboys."

"Where're they?"

He pointed outward, beyond the town. "Out there."

"What are they doing out there?"

"What cowboys do. Punching cows, riding the perimeter to keep intruders off their land. They don't come back till the night most times."

"How many we talking 'bout?"

"Thirty or so. More than there are of us."

"Us who?"

"Townsfolk."

He opened the door a little wider. When I asked him to, he pointed out the different buildings lining the street. There was a general store, café, tailor shop, barbershop, a clothing outfit, a blacksmith's shed, and Chief's cigar shop. He also pointed out Marshal Pewly's jailhouse across the street from the saloon. Doc Watley's clinic was next to that. There were a few towns-folk out now, sweeping the boardwalk in front of their shops, beating rugs, and washing the dust off storefront windows. Otherwise, the town was still eerily quiet.

I instinctively reached into my shirt pocket for a cigarette, and cursed when I found it empty.

"You wantin' a smoke?" Pico said. "I got some."

He pulled a hand-rolled and a match out of his pocket and got me lit.

"You shouldn't smoke, kid."

"I don't," he said. "I just pretend sometimes."

"Usually how it starts." I drew a long drag, savored it. "So what's the deal with this place, Pico?"

"Deal?"

"Well, like, y'all got electricity, telephones?"

He just looked at me.

"How 'bout runnin' water?"

"Sure. Runs right out of the water tower and into the barrels."

"What about that well?" I pointed to the hand-drawn well in the center of town. It was stone-built, about three feet high and ten feet in diameter. Across the top of it spanned a hand-cranked winch wrapped in rusted chain.

"That's gone dry," Pico said. "Been dry as long as I can remember. That's why they built the tower. The tower draws from a much shallower, uh . . . what do you call it?"

"Aquifer?"

"Right. The tower water is milky and don't taste good, but we drink it anyway."

"Big damn water tower for a town this small," I said.

"It's a thirsty place," he said.

"So no commodes?"

"Commodes?"

"Where do you do your business?"

"Outhouse in the back. You need it? There's a lye bucket and scoop over there if you need to do a number."

I told him I didn't.

The largest building in town was on the eastern end, directly across from the water tower.

"That's the boardinghouse," Pico said.

"Got any boarders?"

"Just whores."

"So it's a whorehouse."

"Tilly prefers to call it a boardinghouse."

"Place seemed quiet when I went past it earlier."

"Cowboys'll be coming back at dusk," Pico said. "I'll wake you up before, so we can make a plan. When Cactus Bob tells his brother about you, they'll all come lookin'."

I yawned. "We'll sort it out, Pico. No worries."

"You aren't scared?"

"Scared?" I opened one eye. "Nah. I'm the answer to y'all's prayers, remember?"

He smiled.

I drifted off to the quiet hum of the boy's harmonica.

Once again, my dream came on quick. Once again, it showed it like it really happened.

We were still teenagers.

I can't marry you, Georgia said.

Sure you can, I replied.

She laughed, blew a strand of wet hair from her face, and playfully tried to push me off of her. I playfully resisted, keeping her close, keeping our slick bodies mashed together, staying inside of her.

I kissed her long and hard on the mouth, then asked her why not.

She kissed me back and called me crazy. She told me we'd been going together only two years.

I told her that was plenty long.

She said that we were just eighteen.

I told her that was plenty old.

She said we had no money.

I told her we'd make some.

She giggled and called me one slick charmer.

I agreed that I was, then asked her again to marry me.

She told me I shouldn't have proposed in the backseat of a Chevy because it wasn't romantic.

I reminded her that it was more romantic than a Ford.

She slid out from under me and grabbed her panties and her Dentyne off the rearview mirror, and returned them both to their proper place. She pulled my football jersey back down over her bosoms, slipped back into her cutoffs, and reset her ponytail.

I lit a Salem, pulled up my Levi's, and combed back my hair.

Still shiny with sweat and breathing hard, we rose out of the backseat and sat on the folded-up convertible top, our legs dangling over the seat back.

The Chevy's front wheels were parked at the cliff's edge. The ravine stretched wide before us, just beyond the hood. Below, we could hear the river running swift. Crickets and cicadas screeched all around. Lightning bugs blinked in the woods.

For a time we just sat and listened, touching shoulders, not talking.

I took in the smell of her—cinnamon and lip gloss and sweat.

I looked out over the ravine and thought about what all had happened in the two years since I'd first chased her off the same cliff. The things we'd done. The firsts we'd shared. The fights we'd had. The ways we'd made up.

I thought about Mama dying slowly, and Georgia standing by me through it all.

I flicked away my Salem, half smoked.

Georgia pulled me close and asked what I was thinking.

I told her she knew what I was thinking.

I told her my feelings for her would never change. I told her she was it.

She looked off.

She reminded me that her mother and daddy thought I was sorry and headed nowhere.

I asked if she agreed with that.

She told me that she did.

We stayed quiet for a time.

Then she pivoted toward me, took both my hands, and looked me deep in the eyes.

She asked if I was ever going to hurt her.

I told her I never would.

She made me promise.

I did.

Then she smiled and said, yes I'll marry you, Samuel Parcy Bonham.

She kissed me on the mouth and told me she'd love me forever, too.

9.

I woke up feeling itchy and stiff, and frightened by the fact that my sleep had gone much deeper than the catnap I'd intended.

I felt a wave of panic when I looked outside and saw that dusk had nearly fallen. Firelight was already flickering in the shop windows. There was some relief in seeing that the street was still virtually empty, with only a few townsfolk milling about and no cowboys.

I rubbed my eyes into focus. At my feet were a canteen and a pile of folded clothes with a note atop them: *Clothes and water for you . . . back in a minute with food . . . and a plan!* The note was signed with the letter *P*.

I looked around and saw no sign of the boy. I put the clothes on quick. He'd left brown pants, a brown shirt, a brown vest, and a leather belt. They'd all seen some wear, but they were mostly clean and fit all right. I put on my own boots and Cactus Bob's hat and slung the canteen strap over my shoulder, then hustled down the stairs and crossed to the street-facing side of the stable.

Pegasus was the only horse in the livery. He stood in the

last stall near the door, his nose buried in a bucket of oats. The horse stopped chewing as I passed by. His ears folded back and his hide twitched in a manner that seemed more threatening than defensive. The horse was white, tall, and thick in the neck. His muscled legs were corded with veins. I'd never liked horses. The size of them had always made me nervous. I moved past Pegasus.

The stable opened on a single sliding door. I unlatched it and slid it wide enough to stick my head out. I watched as two townsmen ambled from the barbershop to the general store across the street, and then the street was empty again.

I'd about decided it was time to make my break when the ground began to tremble and there came a strange rumbling sound out of the east. I turned toward the darkened horizon. What I saw knotted my stomach.

The cowboys appeared as silhouettes against the plum sky, riding abreast in a tight formation, driving their steeds hard as dust swirled in their wake. No sooner had I seen them than their hoots and hollers rang out over the drum of pounding hooves and the pop of leather slapping hide.

My body went rigid.

The ground shook harder.

In no time the cowboys were nearing the eastern edge of town. To wait another second would end any chance of escape.

I checked behind me. There was still no sign of Pico. I sprinted across the street, and didn't slow my pace even after getting clear of the town's north side.

I made fifty yards. A hundred. I didn't look back but kept my eyes on the ground, racing across the quarter-mile stretch of plain between the town and the plateau to the north.

I didn't see the horseman standing directly in my path until I nearly ran into him. The sight was so shocking that I hollered out in fright. Against the darkened sky he appeared as a towering silhouette atop the saddle. I didn't bother to question who he was; I merely tried to run around him. When I did, he spurred his horse and cut me off. When I changed direction, he yanked his reins, rounded his horse, and cut me off again. With no other choice, I turned and started back the way I'd come, but managed only a couple of steps before the horseman's lasso fell over me and yanked me backward off my feet. I hit the dirt hard. Pain shot through me.

In my daze I heard the man dismount and approach. When the dust cleared, I found Cactus Bob standing over me, smiling.

"Goin' somewhere, stranger?"

He drove a boot into my gut. Then he ripped his hat off my head and spat tobacco juice in my eye. When I finally recovered my wind and vision, the cowboy led me slowly back toward town, him in the saddle, me on foot behind him, the lasso noose still tight around my chest, pulling me along.

We reentered town on the east side. The sky had gone black. Firelight bathed the street. The corral outside the livery stable was full of lathered horses wallowing in the dirt, freshly free of their saddles. A few people strolled the boardwalks along both sides of the street. I saw no cowboys but heard a racket of music and laughter coming out of the saloon ahead.

I felt the eyes of the townsfolk watching as Cactus Bob proudly led his prize down the middle of the street. I kept my head down, eyes forward, until I heard the shuffle of approaching footsteps. Pico. There were tears streaming down his face.

"You made me a promise, Mr. Searcher, and you broke it."

I said nothing.

"Git on out of here, boy, 'less you want a smackin,'" said Cactus Bob.

Pico stepped back. I moved past him without a look.

As we approached the saloon a cowboy stumbled outside to piss on the hitching post. He pinched off midstream when he saw me and Cactus Bob. His jaw went slack.

"The hell's this?" he asked Cactus Bob.

"Go tell my brother we got us an interloper," said Cactus Bob.

The cowboy looked at me and smiled. Cactus Bob told him to move his ass. The cowboy zipped up and ran back inside.

The music stopped seconds later. A few beats after that a crowd of some thirty cowboys shoved their way outside and fanned out along the boardwalk. Even at a distance they stank. Their faces were red from sun. Their beards were clumped with dust. To a man, they wore boots, spurs, hats, chaps, and six-gun pistols. A few also held rifles.

I eyed them. They eyed me. They kept their silence, save for a few low rumbles of laughter and the odd spin of a Colt cylinder.

The moment stretched.

Movement drew my focus to the second-story window above the saloon. A blurred figure I assumed was Lily Blanca stood in shadow at the parted curtain. Despite the gravity of the situation, or perhaps because of it, her presence had an even more strange and powerful draw on me than before.

The batwing doors clattered again, shifting my attention back. The man Cactus Bob had sent inside came rushing out.

"Red wants to see him!"

"You tell him we'll be right there," said Cactus Bob.

"*Alone*," replied the cowboy.

Cactus Bob's jaw went tight. He spat a defiant stream of black juice, then came down from the saddle. He freed me from the lasso, then spun me around and kicked me hard in the ass. I stumbled forward and fell across the boardwalk steps. The cowboys chuckled as they parted way. I paid them no mind as I got up, dusted off, and stepped inside.

The saloon was still thick with smoke. Tilly sat in her high chair behind the bar, smoking a hand-rolled, showing no expression. Calvin was at the piano, his back to the room, his hands resting on his knees. I saw no one else in the room.

I asked Tilly for a whiskey.

The barmaid didn't move. The saloon was still and quiet.

"Give it to him."

The deep voice had spoken out of the darkness at the back of the room.

I moved to the bar. Tilly poured the whiskey slowly. I drank it fast, then I pointed for another.

"I told you not to leave," Tilly said under her breath, keeping her eyes on the glass between us.

"Figure I got a habit of doin' things my own way," I said.

She poured the second shot.

"Bring it," said the voice in the back.

I didn't bring it. I belted it right there, hoping it might bring me a little calm and a lot of courage.

I moved through the curtain of smoke toward the back. Red Danyon sat alone at a corner table, his face hidden beneath the wide brim of his hat. Only a square, stubbled jaw and thin

throat. "Don't be so jumpy, Searcher." He poured two fingers of whiskey into the extra glass and held it out to me. "I merely wanted to welcome you to my town is all."

I didn't trust what he'd said, but I wanted the whiskey, so I mirrored his smile and played along.

"In that case I'm much obliged." I took the glass, raised it to him, belted the shot, then turned toward the piano at my back. "Say, Calvin, how 'bout a little 'Red River Valley'?"

The piano stayed silent.

Guns cocked behind me. I turned back around. Danyon stood slowly, his twin Colts aimed at my chest.

"This is me playing with myself, Searcher."

The shot glass slipped from my fingers. I looked down the long barrels of the guns.

"Word is you know how to use those things," I said.

Danyon smiled. He aimed one of the guns toward the bar, on which stood eight half-drunk glasses of beer. Tilly ducked. Danyon fired six quick shots.

Then there were two glasses on the bar.

Danyon twirled the smoking gun and slid it home. He kept the other one aimed at me.

Spurs rattled as he stepped forward and pressed the gun between my eyes. "One thing I didn't tell you about those pawns, Searcher. Sometimes they have to be sacrificed to ensure the survival of the king. You hate to give 'em up, but then . . . well, the greater good and all that. Let's walk."

With his gun poking hard at my back, Danyon nudged me outside. The rest of the cowboys were still scattered on or around the boardwalk, spitting and smoking and fiddling with their weapons. Beyond them, the townsfolk were gathered in a tight cluster in the middle of the street.

Every head turned when we came out. Every voice went silent.

"String a rope," Danyon said.

10.

I saw a couple of familiar faces in the crowd, Chief and Marshal Pewly among them. The marshal had a hand on the butt of his toy pistol, looking like he thought he should be doing something, but not knowing what. Doc Watley was also there, red in his eyes, a bottle of sour mash in his hand.

The rest of the townsfolk ran the gamut of your basic boomtown workforce. They all looked worn down by hard living. The men had sweat-stained shirts and pants with holes. A few of them held fiery torches in their callused hands. Most of the women wore handmade dresses and their hair in buns, except for the whores, who were dressed for work in satin and lace. I saw only a half-dozen whores, not many given the number of cowboys in town.

The only thing I didn't see any of were kids, other than Pico, who stood at the front of the group, his cheeks still wet with tears.

Danyon shoved me hard from behind, and I stumbled down off the boardwalk. As soon as my feet hit the dirt, Cactus Bob tripped me up again, and I toppled to the ground. The cowboys laughed as I coughed in a cloud of dust. A swift kick in the ass from Cactus Bob brought me quickly back to my feet.

The shove-and-trip routine continued down the street, until I wound up on all fours on the west side of town, staring at a noose that had already been slung over the sign spanning the town entrance.

The sudden inevitability of my death struck me with cold fear. All the confidence and composure I'd felt inside the saloon had escaped me.

I stood and wiped the dirt from my cuts and scrapes. One of the cowboys rolled a barrel out from under the water tower and set a milking stool down beside it. Red Danyon used the stool to step up onto the barrel to be seen above the crowd. The tail of his duster fluttered in the wind as he extended a hand in my direction.

"As you all know by now, Mr. Searcher here has broken the law of the land. He entered . . . and he left. Perhaps we owe him a debt of gratitude for reminding us that such an offense will always incur swift and just punishment."

Another cowboy placed a coiled bullwhip in Danyon's extended hand.

Cactus Bob stepped up and shackled my wrists behind me. "I'm gonna enjoy watching you stretch, you sumbitch," he said.

A horse trotted up next to me, led by two cowboys on foot. It was Pegasus.

"No!" Pico shouted. The boy tried to break from the crowd, but a couple of the townsmen held him back.

Pegasus stomped in the dirt, clearly distressed. As more cowboys moved in to hold the horse's reins, two others hoisted me onto the saddle. Pegasus jerked his head in protest. His ears folded back.

Looking again at the whip in Danyon's hand, I began to

realize how it was all going to happen. There'd be no gallows. No trapdoor. Just a pissed-off horse running out from under me and letting me swing. Trouble was, that also meant no hard fall. Which meant no instant death.

A sickening feeling came over me.

"Listen, Danyon," I said, hearing the panic in my own voice. "Only reason I wound up here is that I got lost trying to find Mexico. I meant to disappear there forever and never be found. Whatever you got going on here is no concern of mine. You let me go, and I'll swear on my dead mother's name I ain't never heard of this place. Just don't let me swing!"

A few of the cowboys snickered at my pleas. The laughter was infectious. Soon they were all chuckling.

Red Danyon offered no reaction.

The townsfolk circled in closer. Their faces were orange in the firelight. I saw a few heads shaking, but otherwise I saw little expression from any of them. There seemed to be an element of routine to what was happening. I got the idea this wasn't the first hanging they'd been witness to. Only Pico was showing emotion. The boy was crying hysterically now, much more for the sake of his horse, I was sure, than for me.

Danyon signaled his men. Two cowboys led me and Pegasus into position under the noose. The loop was set and secured at my throat.

Panic took hold. I squirmed in the saddle, fighting against the shackles at my wrists.

"Goddamnit, Danyon, don't do this!"

Danyon stepped down from the barrel and relit his cigar.

I caught movement outside the saloon in the distance. Calvin pushed through the flapping doors cradling Tilly in his

11.

The beating had been short, but effective. My bottom lip had busted open. My nose had swollen so tight that it whistled when I breathed. Every muscle in my body hurt. Perhaps the worst pain of all was the rope burn around my neck. Of course I'd received no medical treatment before being tossed into a cell.

There were two rooms to the jailhouse. The main room was square and stark, with a dusty planked floor. The only furnishings were Marshal Pewly's large wooden desk and a straight-back chair. Behind the desk hung an old map of Texas, back when Texas belonged to the Mexicans. On the opposite wall was a gun rack that held no guns.

The cell room was just off the main room. There was only one cell, about six by ten feet, with bars on two sides. The only amenities were a wooden cot, a cornhusk mattress, and a folding chair.

I'd been licking my wounds in the cell for more than an hour when Marshal Pewly, under the watchful eye of two armed cowboys, stepped into the room with the big man from the box in their custody. By all appearances, the man who'd saved my life had received a beating to match my own. Both of his eyes were purple and swollen. A trickle of blood ran down one corner of his mouth. He seemed to be struggling for balance. I was glad to see that someone had at least given him some clothes.

The marshal unlocked the cell door. The old man ducked his head and entered without resistance.

"Pewly, you big dumb buzzard," said one of the cowboys to the marshal. "Think you got brains enough to keep watch on these two sumbitches?"

"I'm not the marshal around here for nothing," answered Pewly with pride.

The cowboys cackled at that, then staggered drunkenly out of the building.

Marshal Pewly paled, embarrassed by the taunts. He looked at me through the bars. "I'm real sorry about this, Mr. Searcher. But I'm told it's just for the night. Word is they're letting you two out in the morning to put you to work. Y'all just let me know if you need anything."

He moved into the other room and took a seat behind his desk.

The old man was still standing just inside the cell door. I rose from my seat on the cot and gestured for him to take my place. He moved to it in a strange, hip-swaying gait. The journey across the cramped cell left him winded. The cot creaked under his weight. With a heavy sigh, he pressed his back against the wall.

"You all right?" I asked.

"I'll live."

"Looks like they gave you a good wallop."

"Those cowhands don't know what a wallop is." He spat blood on the floor. "*Yet.*"

There was a distinctive rhythm to his voice. The words came out slow and stretched and sort of clipped at the end. He pulled a cigarette and a match from his hip pocket and struck the match on the wall behind him.

"Where'd you get the smoke?" I asked.

"Made a friend."

He looked at me. After a few beats he pulled out another cigarette and offered it. We both got lit. I took a seat in the chair across from him. We smoked in silence for a time.

"That was some rifle shot," I finally said.

"Wasn't nothing."

"Was to me. What if you'd missed?"

"Never occurs to me to miss."

"Well, anyway, I guess I should thank you. You sure didn't have to do it. For all you knew I was some no-good swindler who had that hanging coming."

"You're right." He peered at me through smoke. "I did it for the horse."

I shifted uncomfortably in the chair.

"Who gave you the clothes?" I asked.

"Same friend," he said. "The Mexican kid. Taco."

"Pico," I corrected.

The clothes were much too small for the big man. The brown work pants hit him at midcalf. The sleeves of his ratty peasant shirt barely reached his elbows. He was still barefoot.

"So I take it that rifle had fallen out of the airplane, too, huh?"

Truth is, my memory's a bit shaky." He shook his head. "Damn horse."

"Horse?"

"I reckon he bucked me again. Last thing I remember is seeing Aaron's homestead on the horizon."

"Aaron?"

"My brother." He made a rueful chuckle. "Been traveling three years to reach him, finally had his place in my sights and then . . . nothing. That's all I remember. Next thing I know, I'm wandering blind through the desert."

I considered this. "You really don't remember anything about that airplane?"

"I'll ask you one more time, friend, what's an airplane?"

I offered no answer. We smoked them down. He lit another.

"Well, anyway . . ." I said. "Has anyone told you the way it works here yet? Law of the land and all that?"

He nodded. "The kid told me."

I scooted my chair forward and lowered my voice. "Between us, I aim to get hell and gone of this town, law or no law. Care to share your plans?"

"I'm ridin' out to find Aaron, like I told ya."

"I figured. So from where I sit, you and me might best work together."

"Worth a thought, I reckon."

"Safety in numbers and all that."

Smoke left his mouth. "There'll be safety in you doin' exactly as I say when I say it."

The comment took me aback. "Now, I'm not sure you gotta put it that—"

"We'll start by going after the Winchester," he said.

"How come us to do that?"

"I reckon I take out a few of those cowhands with the rifle, we'll be able to get our hands on some six-guns."

"Guns? Why guns?"

He looked as though it'd been a stupid question. "Well, we're not just gonna use harsh language."

"Why make noise? I say we wait till the wee hours, when the cowboys are good and drunk, then sneak off while it's still dark."

"Sneak off?"

"Escape."

"Escape?" His jaw went tight. "I ain't escaping nothin.'"

I sat back in the chair. "Maybe I didn't hear you right. I thought you aimed to go see your brother."

"That's right."

"Well, they ain't just gonna let you stroll outta here with a packed lunch and a fare-thee-well. Remember the law of the land?"

"I do. And I aim to put an end to it."

"How you figure on doing that?"

"By killin' every cowhand in this town."

"You mind repeatin' that?"

"You heard me."

"What would you do that for?"

"Ya mean aside from the beating they gave me? Haven't ya seen the faces on them poor folks out there, living under the fear of the gun? The kid told me all about it. One man leaves, another man hangs for it. That's how they keep those folks from runnin' off. Well, I ain't gonna run and be the cause of an innocent man's hangin,' I'll tell ya that. These people need my help. I aim to give it to 'em."

"Oh yeah? Why you?"

"'Cause that's the way I'm built." He dropped his cigarette and crushed it under his bare foot. His eyes came up slowly. "What exactly are *you* built of?"

"Good sense, I figure. Sense enough not to do some damn fool thing like you're talkin' 'bout."

"Fool thing, hell. I've faced down Yankee battalions that'd make the cowhands out there look like a band of schoolmarms."

I shrugged. "Well, fine then. Long as you aim to shoot up the place, I'd appreciate it if you'd shoot down any more nooses that get strung up on account of my leavin'. 'Cause that's what I'm doin'."

We held gazes.

The side of his mouth curved in a wry smile. "Settle down, friend, you're getting jumpy."

"I'm settled. And I ain't your friend."

"What's your name?"

"They call me Searcher."

"So tell me, Searcher, ya think you can take that desert on your—"

He winced. His hand moved quickly to his stomach. I asked him what was wrong.

"Bellyache is all." He winced again, then waited until the pain passed. He took a breath. "Where was I?"

"The desert."

"Ya think you can take that desert alone?"

"Done it before."

"Not with armed horsemen on your trail. Those cowhands'll

aim to follow you, ya know?" He looked me up and down. "Little fella like you? Somehow I ain't so sure you could hack it."

"Little fella? Look here, Edwards . . . you keep talking like that, and I'll make sure your next words are your last."

"That'll be the day . . ."

"And another thing. Long as we're—" I stopped. "What did you just say?"

"I said that'll be the day. You and me in a tussle? Why, I could whup you to a frazzle."

That'll be the day. The notion that had suddenly popped into my head after hearing him say those words hit me like a punch to the gut.

"Ya got a strange look on your face, Searcher. What's eatin' ya?"

"Morrison . . ." I whispered. "*Marion Morrison . . .*"

"You call me by that name again, and we really will have words."

I looked up slowly. My hand rose to cover my open mouth.

"You'd best take 'er easy there, Pilgrim," he said. "Ya look like ya seen a ghost."

I found myself unable to speak.

The old man shrugged, then leaned his head back against the wall and shut his eyes.

I'd gone dry-mouthed and dizzy.

I stood, turning my back to him, and placed my head against the bars. My mind went into a frenzy, putting pieces together.

"It's not possible," I said, thinking aloud. "It can't be possi—"

The sound of the man's droning snore turned me around. He was out cold.

"Can we talk?" I asked.

It was a few moments before he'd even look at me. When he did his gaze was cold.

"Upstairs," he said.

We sat on the floor of the loft, in the same spot we'd been the day before. He poured me a tin cup of water. I drank the cup dry and thanked him.

"First things first," I said. "I'm sorry 'bout runnin' out on you yesterday evening. And I'm damn sorry about your horse. He gonna be okay?"

"In time."

"You done good with that horse, Pico. I figure he saved my life."

"Forget it."

"I ain't gonna. Ever. And I can promise you right now, I won't go behind your back again."

The boy just shrugged. It wasn't forgiveness, but I figured it was a start.

"You wanted to talk?"

I nodded. "Got some things in my head need sorting out. You being a kid, without all the imagination schooled out of you, I figure you might be the only one to believe me."

"What is it?"

I took a breath to compose my thoughts, not quite sure where to start. "You ever seen a movie, Pico? A picture show?"

He shook his head. "Heard talk of 'em, though. Tilly's mentioned them a time or two."

"Well, as a boy I loved old movies. And my favorites were Western pictures—movies about cowboys. My daddy had boxes full of these old Western pictures on videotape. He collected 'em, see. And after Daddy left, I found his collection up in the attic and kept it for my own."

"Where'd your daddy go?"

"At the time, I didn't know. Matter of fact, I didn't find out for years . . . but if it's all the same, Pico, that's a subject I wouldn't care to get into. All that matters is he left, back when I was about your age. And after he left, I watched his old Western films all the time, over and over, till I knew 'em frame for frame. Those movie cowboys were like heroes to me. In fact, I figure they became about the closest thing to family I had, besides my mama."

"What's this got to do with me?" asked Pico.

"Well, there was this one movie cowboy who was bigger and better than all the rest. He'd been Daddy's favorite, which made him my favorite, too. I haven't seen any of his films since I was a kid, 'cause I've long since put childhood stuff behind me. Buried it, you might say. Still, I figure this particular movie cowboy made quite a mark on me, 'cause as I think on him now, a lot of his films still come back with good clarity. This man was quite the presence, you see. He's been missed by people the world over."

"Missed? What happened to him?"

"He died."

"Oh."

"Point is . . ." I took another deep breath and looked Pico in the eye. "I think this actor I'm talking about is the man who shot that hanging rope last night to save my life."

The boy showed neither shock nor disbelief, leading me to think that maybe I was talking to the right person after all.

"Mr. Edwards?" he said. "What makes you think he's a famous dead movie cowboy?"

"Few things. Now, I'm just thinking out loud here, so bear with me. But if I'm right about all this, and not just plumb crazy, that man's real name isn't Ethan Edwards . . . it's John Wayne."

"John who?"

"John Wayne. And from your expression, I'm guessing that name don't mean much to you."

Pico said it didn't.

"Well, it's important to know that John Wayne was sometimes called Duke, and sometimes even called *The* Duke. And like I said, back when I was your age, the man meant just about everything to me. See, Duke always played the hero. The good guy. The odds were always stacked against him, but nobody ever got the best of him in the end. With Daddy gone, Duke became the man I looked up to most, the man I hoped to become. So I learned everything about him that I could."

"Like what?"

"Well, for example, Duke's mama didn't name him John Wayne. His given name was Marion Morrison."

"Why'd his mama give him a girl's name?"

"One wonders," I said.

Pico looked off in thought, then came back. "Back up a minute, Mr. Searcher. Assuming that what you're saying is even possible, how'd this man wind up in Blistered Valley?"

I passed the next few minutes recounting everything about the plane crash, the man with one arm, and the big silver box. Pico took it all in without interruption, then thumbed his lip for a few moments, thinking.

"And Mr. Edwards just popped right out, huh?"

"Popped right out," I said. "Naked as a jaybird."

"And tell me again why you thought he was this dead movie star?"

"I didn't at first. I didn't start putting all this together until last night in the jailhouse, when the man started spoutin' off about the Civil War, and talkin' in quotes from his own movies. Hearing those lines spoken in that voice—one of the most recognizable voices of all time—well, I was struck. Once I started thinking on it all, one thought led to another."

"What thoughts?"

"Well for starters, the name Marion Morrison was written on the underside of that box's lid. And below that was a date. June 11, 1979. And that just happens to be the date that John Wayne died."

"Still, that doesn't exactly mean—"

"Doesn't mean squat," I said. "Until you put it with everything else. See, in my studies of the man, I remember learning that Duke had had a sick lung removed because he smoked too much. Well, when the old man crawled out of the box, I noticed a zipperlike scar on his chest."

"I saw it, too," Pico said, "when he was getting dressed. He also had a scar just like it on his belly."

"That's right, he—" I stopped. "Hot damn, Pico, you're right! I'd forgotten all about the one on his stomach! This backs up my case even more. You know what Duke died of?"

"How could I?"

"Stomach cancer! Kind of makes me think that at some point he had his tummy cut open by a doctor. That would explain the second scar."

"Also might explain the bellyache he complained of last night."

seemed like a tangle of mixed wires. No matter which way I spun it, the whole thing still seemed ridiculous.

On the other hand, there were two things I was certain of: the man from the box *did* have The Duke's walk and he *did* have The Duke's talk. Like any barroom regular, I'd seen my share of John Wayne impressions, and they all boiled down to one thing—nobody does The Duke like The Duke. "But how come no one else recognized him?" I asked, thinking aloud.

"What's that, Mr. Searcher?"

"Surely Doc Watley and Marshal Pewly, hell all those cowboys, would have recognized him. I mean, they weren't born here, were they?"

"Only person born in this town is me," Pico said.

"That's my point. The rest of those folks would know The Duke anywhere. I'm telling you, Pico, there ain't a person alive who wouldn't know this guy."

"Does he still look like he did in the picture shows?"

I thought about it. "Not really. Not at all, in fact."

"What's different?"

"Aside from him being all wrinkled and sagged? He used to have hair, for one thing, or at least a passable toupee. But also, those cowboys roughed him up something fierce. His face is pretty damn purple and swollen. Thinking on it that way, it makes sense no one recognized him."

"I believe you're overthinkin' it, Mr. Searcher."

"How so?"

"Why *would* anyone think that old man was the real Duke? They all think he's been dead for thirty years. There's also the fact that he'd be . . . how old now?"

I attempted the math. "Well, over a hundred, anyway."

"So there you go. The man looks old, but not *that* old."

Pico was making some good sense.

"So what now?" he said. "Shouldn't we tell somebody?"

"Who . . . and what for? First, we don't know that it's true. Second, we start spouting this John Wayne is risen business, and the whole town'll think we've been grazin' in the locoweed. Way I see it, we best keep this between us, Pico. And there's another thing I should tell you, too."

"What?"

"I think Duke'll be dead by week's end."

"What makes you say that?"

"He's planning a suicide mission. He told me as much in the jailhouse. He thinks he's gonna kill all those cowboys for beating on him."

"Kill them? Which ones."

"All of 'em. Said he aims to get hold of that Winchester again, go Rambo on every damn cowpuncher out there. He confided the whole thing to me."

"He confided?" Pico's eyes lit up. "So then you're gonna help him?"

"The hell I am. He wants to launch Operation Gunsmoke, he'll be doing it alone."

"But why would he need to do it alone when he's got you? And I'll help, too. Together, we could make Blistered Valley what it used to be!"

"Pico, don't even start in on that again. We wouldn't have a chance. Me and you are a couple of scrawnies. And Duke is—"

"The greatest cowboy hero of all time! That's what you *said*. You said no one ever got the best of him."

"On-screen sure, but that's in the movies. This is real life."

Cactus Bob pulled his pistol and aimed it at my stomach. "How 'bout we just find out?"

The other cowboys shared a giggle.

Duke stayed quiet.

I cut my eyes toward the corral and saw almost more dung in it than dirt. The horses had been cleared. I turned and looked down the length of the street. Most of the cowboys were already on the range, leaving just a skeleton crew behind.

"Why can't we just pile and burn it right here?" I asked Cactus Bob.

"'Cause I wanna watch your ass haul shit in the hot sun, that's why."

The cowboys climbed the corral fence, sat, and lit smokes.

Me and Duke went to work without sharing a word.

After two hours, we'd each made more than a dozen round trips across town, wheeling heavy loads. My hands turned raw with blisters. My strength was sapped.

Two of the cowboys had sauntered off not long after we'd started, having wilted in the heat. One cowboy stayed behind with Cactus Bob to chaperone. They'd started cutting their thirst with whiskey around midmorning, and they were good and lathered by the time Cactus Bob raised his head and hollered, "What the hell do you think you're doing, old man?"

I stopped shoveling and turned. Duke had taken it upon himself to drop his shovel and light up a smoke.

Whiskey jug in hand, Cactus Bob came down off the fence and ambled toward him.

Duke carried on smoking.

The air grew thick with tension.

Cactus Bob spat a stream of black juice and stepped up square with Duke. "I asked you a question, old man: What the hell you doin'?"

Duke took a defiant drag off his hand-rolled, staggered his feet, and hooked his thumbs at the waist of his pants. He eyed Cactus Bob up and down. "Reckon I'm just picking my moment," he said.

At first Cactus Bob looked confused. Then he laughed. He said to the cowboy on the fence behind him, "You hear that, Jasper? The old man's picking his moment."

Jasper joined in the laughter.

With a hooked finger, Cactus Bob hoisted his whiskey jug onto his shoulder. He bit the cork out and spat it, then tipped the jug and took a healthy pull. He raked a sleeve over his wet beard. "Picking your moment for what, you old shit ass?"

Duke said nothing.

The other cowboy, Jasper, came down from the fence and joined the face-off.

I kept my distance.

The corral went still and silent. Seconds passed.

Then Cactus Bob backhanded Duke across the cheek.

Duke's face held like stone. He drew a slow breath, then flicked his smoke away and rubbed a hand over the reddened part of his face.

The jug fell from Cactus Bob's hand.

"Looks like I've found my moment," Duke said.

Cactus Bob's nostrils flared. "You wanna swing on me, old man, why don't you go ahead and—"

Duke did.

Or at least he tried to.

Cactus Bob ducked the punch with nearly a full second to spare. By the time Duke had lumbered into his follow-through, Cactus Bob had already come back up and driven a hard fist into Duke's gut.

I winced. The sight was as painful as it was pathetic.

Duke doubled over, then dropped to his hands and knees, struggling to draw breath. Jasper stepped in and drove a fist into the small of the old man's back. Then Cactus Bob jabbed a spur into Duke's thigh. A half minute passed before Duke's head finally came up. His eyes found me through the dust.

Cactus Bob followed Duke's gaze. "You care to step in here for your little friend, Searcher? Come on, we'll kick your ass fair and square."

Cactus Bob undid his gun belt and tossed it away. Jasper followed suit. Both men raised their fists.

Duke's eyes stayed on me.

"What are you waiting for, Searcher . . .?"

The voice had come from behind me. I spun around. Red Danyon stood just outside the corral fence, rolling his cigar over a match flame.

"Go ahead," he said. "You have my blessing."

I met eyes with each man around me in turn, then shook my head. "I got no quarrel here."

Duke's face fell again. He rolled onto his back, still fighting to breathe.

"Jasper, cart this old git down to Doc Watley's," Cactus Bob said. "I figure he's done been broke for the day. Searcher, you get your short ass back to work."

Jasper lifted Duke from the dirt and slung him facedown across one of the wheelbarrows, already half full of dung. He started off down the road. Red Danyon fell into step behind him, puffing cigar smoke and quietly laughing to himself. Cactus Bob went to retrieve the gun belts.

I turned and went back for my shovel. In my periphery, I caught Pico standing just inside the stable door. Our eyes met. He turned and headed back into the shadows.

"So, ya fast with a gun or not?"

"I'm fast, but I figure I got lucky with Cactus Bob. Don't figure to be so lucky a second time."

"Maybe ya got more in ya than ya think."

"More what?"

"Grit, maybe."

"Only grit I got is under my toenails. Sorry, Duke, but I ain't the hero type. If it'll help convince you, I'll add that I'm also an outlaw on the run."

"Name's Edwards, not Duke, and what's your being an outlaw got to do with it?"

"Means only two things could come of my hanging around Blistered Valley. Either the law will eventually find me here and cart me off to my doom, or I'll live out the rest of my days shoveling Danyon's shit for sport. Between the two choices, I'll take Mexico."

"I'm offering you another choice."

"There ain't one."

He pounded the table. "You can fight!"

The music stopped. All heads turned our way. Me and Duke held eyes over the glow of the coal-oil lamp, waiting out the reprieve.

When the room was bustling again, I said, "Look, I don't know what Pico told you, but—"

"He told me he sees something in you ya don't see in yourself."

"Well, he's wrong. And my life will be a whole lot simpler soon as I'm rid of that damn boy."

Duke blew another smoke ring. "That what you thought when you ran out on your own boy?"

I looked up, certain I'd heard him wrong. "What did you say to me, old man?"

"You heard me."

"I don't think I did."

He crushed out his smoke. His eyes stayed on me. "Maybe you best just keep on running, Searcher, from everyone and everything. Sure seems to be working for ya so far."

My hands formed fists on the table. "How did you—"

"Ya talk in your sleep. Fella can learn a lot about a man by listening to him dream."

"I think you and me are done here." I scooted back my chair and stood.

"Yer right, Searcher . . ." His tone had changed suddenly. His voice sounded distant, weaker. His eyes peered up slowly. "I *am* sick. And I *am* old. And somewhere along the line, my whole damn life passed me by. The young man I knew myself to be is gone. I don't look the same. Don't feel the same. And I sure as hell can't fight the same. And whatever sickness is eatin' at my gut is eatin' at the rest of me, too. I'm certain of it . . . just as certain as the turnin' of the earth." He finished his whiskey and rose from the chair. He stood square with me. "I may not be long in this world, but I got one more fight left in me. I may be old and wore-out, but I still got know-how, and I still got dead aim. What I don't have is strength, speed . . . and *time*. Way I see it, you got all three." He spat on the floor at my feet. "Just a damn shame you don't have the backbone to put 'em to good use."

15.

It was a half hour later.

Me and Duke had parted ways to do our drinking from different ends of the saloon. I took a table in a far corner. Duke remained where he was, keeping his head low and his glass filled. Our conversation had left me hot. It was one thing to question my grit. It was another to talk about my boy out of turn. The novelty of the man's being topside in this world again had already long worn off.

Time passed. Whiskey flowed. Poker chips bounced. Spittoons pinged. I'd just started in on another whiskey/beer combo when a booming voice jarred the room.

"Goddamn it, Pico!"

A hush swept the saloon. Red Danyon was standing midway down the stairs, his gun drawn and pointed at Pico, who was still sitting at the end of the bar. Danyon thumbed the trigger. "You blow that fuckin' thing again, boy, I'll shoot your lips off!"

Pico paled and lowered the harmonica from his mouth. "You weren't in the room," he said. "I didn't think—"

There was laughter.

"Fine then, ya big fee-male, go ahead and leave. But I'm keepin' yer winnin's!"

The saloon door shut.

I went back to work.

Denver Mack had jug ears, a moon face, and jowls like a bulldog. He also smelled like a bulldog. He was taller than me, but only just. I stripped the man to his long johns, then slipped into his clothes. The cowboy's hat was too big, which was good because it sat low over my eyes. Unfortunately, it appeared that he'd left his pistol and gun belt at the poker table.

I headed back inside. Good thing was, walking drunk with your head down and your hat low wasn't the sort of thing that drew much attention inside Tilly's. I weaved my way through the crowded tables and chairs, stumbling here and there for effect.

I made it to the base of the stairs without incident, but took a moment to scan the room to make sure I wasn't being watched.

Duke sat alone as before, sipping whiskey, looking downtrodden. Chief was slumped before his beer at the bar. Doc Watley was shuffling the domino boneyard as Marshal Pewly looked on from across the table. Tilly was pouring them quick as she could for Red Danyon and his inner circle, which now included Cactus Bob. The men had their backs to me.

I pulled Denver Mack's hat down low, brought his bandanna up over my nose bandit style, then headed up the stairs. At the top were just a small landing, a closed door, and a lazy-eyed cowboy.

He sat with his chair tilted back against Lily Blanca's door, his boots propped up on the opposite wall. A cigarette dangled from his bottom lip. He carried a six-gun on each hip.

"Wake up there, partner!" I drew finger pistols off my hips, like a child doing a quick draw.

The cowboy jumped, startled, and squinted his eyes to find focus. He looked unamused. He also looked unsober.

"That you, Carl?" he said.

"Guess again, cow chip."

"Cheever?"

"Not even close."

"Ah, hell . . ." He rubbed his watered eyes and squinted some more. "Oh . . . Denver Mack . . . shoulda known. Fuck you want?"

"Found a rat in the shithouse," I said. "Wondered if I might borrow a gun. I'd use my own, but I left it under a whore's bed."

He shrugged and held out one of his Colts. I took it by the barrel and whacked his skull with the handle. He slumped back into the chair, out cold. I pulled his hat down over his eyes and slipped his gun back into its holster.

Then I headed into Lily Blanca's room and shut the door behind me.

16.

Darkness greeted me . . . along with a hard knock to the head.

"Christ!" I said.

Broken glass rained down from my hat brim.

"Get out!"

"Christ!" I said again, hobbling around blindly.

"Which one are you?"

"It's Sam!"

A hand slapped my face. "Sam who?"

"Bonham!"

Another slap.

"I mean Searcher!"

"*Searcher?*"

"Yeah Searcher, goddamnit, quit hittin' me!"

A match lit.

Two figures stood before me in the faint light. They were both Lily Blanca. I asked what in Christ's name was the matter with her.

"I thought you were one of them."

"That was the idea."

"I'm so sorry!"

The match went out. She led me through the darkness to the edge of what felt like a bed. She took a seat beside me, and I heard her fiddling with another match. The room still smelled of heated sex. I took off Denver Mack's hat and rubbed at the welt rising on my head.

"Damn, woman, what'd you whack me with?"

"Flower vase."

"Christ."

"Don't blaspheme."

Another match flared, and she brought it up between us. The sight of her stole my breath. Her eyes were deep brown. Her lips were plush red. Her hair was dark and curly and worn pinned up, exposing her neck.

She wore a white silk robe, opened low across the chest and tied at the waist. Her olive complexion was flawless, save for a long red scar that ran snakelike from her left ear, across her cheek, and down to the base of her chin. It was a knife wound, years old, which had healed without the benefit of proper stitching. I'd seen enough of them in my barroom experience to recognize it. The scar was hard to look past, yet took nothing away from her beauty.

I was still gazing at her when the second match flamed out.

She leaned across my lap to reach a lamp on the nightstand. Even her sweat smelled good. She put a flame in the lamp, and the walls lit with a soft glow.

The room had that typical Old West bordello feel to it. The color scheme was maroon and black. Fringe hung anywhere it could. The bedspread and pillows were satin. Beneath a cracked oval mirror on the far wall was a vanity cluttered with pewter brushes, hand mirrors, and squeeze-bulb bottles of perfume.

Lily set the lamp on the floor at her feet. Her hair caught the light, like a halo. To look at her was to view a clash between righteous purity and sexual fantasy.

The combination was as confusing as it was alluring.

I flinched as she brought a hand up to my face. She smiled, then gently pulled Denver Mack's bandanna down off my nose.

"You should've removed this before coming in," she said. "Might have saved you a knock on the head."

"Did it to fool the guard outside. At least no one knows I'm here."

"If they did, you'd be dead already."

"You figure?"

She nodded. "And so do you. So why *did* you risk coming up?"

"Figure it's best I don't tell you on a dry throat."

She moved to a chest of drawers festooned with hosiery. Atop the dresser were a whiskey decanter and some clean glasses. She poured two fingers for each of us and returned to the bed beside me.

I sipped my drink. It was good liquor, thick and warm. "I'm guessing this is Red Danyon's private stock?"

"That could be said of everything in this room."

"Even you, right?" I took another drink. "He give you that scar?"

She looked down at her glass. "You were about to tell me why you came up here."

"Figured it was high time we met. In fact, I felt it was my God-given duty to come up."

"Well, hell, don't go overboard on the gratitude," I said. I poured another two fingers of whiskey, enjoying the hum it was bringing to my back teeth. I raised the glass to my lips, but paused before drinking it. "You *do* believe me, don't you?"

She crossed to the window and looked outside, her face drawn in thought.

"Yes," she said. "If you tell me the man downstairs is the real Wayne, I believe you. And yes, it is a miracle." She looked back at me. "But he is not the man I prayed for."

"Oh, he ain't? Well, who else could you possibly want?"

"You."

"Trust me, you're better off with The Duke."

"I asked for a cowboy."

"Well, maybe you're not schooled on such things, but ask around. You ain't gonna get more cowboy than John Goddamn Wayne."

"You're not hearing me," she said. "I asked for a *cowboy* . . . not an actor."

"What makes you think I'm a cowboy?"

"You told me you were."

"If I told you I was the tooth fairy, would you believe that, too?"

"I can feel it in my heart. And the Lord doesn't play tricks with—"

"Lily, I'm a pool hustler and drywall man. I'm also a husband and a father. And I've failed at every damn one of those pursuits. What part of 'I'm no good' ain't gettin' through your righteous skull?"

"I'm not saying you've done good, Mr. Searcher . . . but I see good in you just the same."

"Well, thanks for that." I belted the whiskey. "But I'm still leaving this town."

"You leave, and others will die."

"Nah, Duke aims to prevent that. He's really got it in for these cowboys, you'll take comfort to know."

"But we need *you*. You must help us!"

There was desperation in her voice now.

I looked at her. We held a long stare.

Suddenly, her expression changed. Her eyes fell, and her features softened. She reached up and let her hair fall down across her shoulders. There was some sway in her walk as she started coming toward me.

"What will it take, Mr. Searcher? Tell me, and it's yours. I'll give you whatever you want."

"How 'bout the freedom to leave? Maybe a canteen or two and a sack lunch before I head out."

"Anything," she whispered. "Just ask me, and it's yours."

She untied her robe and parted it. Underneath she wore a tight purple corset with matching ruffled britches. Her stockings were red silk. She stepped forward until we were face-to-face. Her eyes peered up. She made her lips wet. Her hands rose to my chest, then crept up and around my neck.

I swallowed.

"Anything," she whispered again. "Anything at all."

She kissed me.

I made to resist, but gave in quick.

Our bodies met. Our hips pressed together firm, and our tongues tangled. My hands moved inside the robe, slipped around her waist, then moved down over her bottom to the backs of her thighs. I went hard and pulled her against me. She took a fistful of my hair and tipped my head back. She kissed her way down my neck, her tongue leaving warm slicks on my skin. I was well on my way to bringing it home, when some strange force compelled me to jerk away.

I stepped back, breathing heavy.

We looked at each other. Her face shone with sweat.

I moved to the dresser, belted two quick shots, then stumbled past her to the vanity across the room.

"What's wrong?" she asked.

"*It's* wrong," I said. "No use pretending it ain't." My eyes went up to the mirror. I looked hard at the man staring back. "Like I said, Lily, I'm married . . . to a fine woman. I'm also daddy to a good boy. I think I'm dead to 'em both. They all but said as much to my face a few days back, but . . ." My gaze fell. I shook my head. "Well, once upon a time I told my wife she'd be the only one for me. Standing here with you now, I figure I must've really meant it."

Lily Blanca retied her robe and wrapped her arms over her chest. "I'm sorry. I should never have—"

"Ain't your fault," I said. "What just happened took two. And Lord knows I've been speculatin' on it since you first spoke my name. Anyway . . . I'm not lost on the fact that your motives weren't entirely romantic."

She didn't argue the point.

I stumbled to the bed, lit another cigarette, and inhaled deeply. The whiskey had left my body numb. My words were coming out slurred.

"I'm sorry if I disappoint you," I said.

"You don't."

"Well, I should." I looked up slowly. "I'm a murderer, Lily. I

ran out on my family for months on a damn fool's errand . . .
came back to see that a decent man had taken my place, and in
a blind drunk I killed him. Now I got that to live with. Got it
to die with, too, I figure."

If what I'd said had made her uneasy, she didn't show it.

"There is still hope for you," she said. "There's always grace."

"Not for me, there ain't. But it's okay. I accept it."

"Well, I don't."

I chuckled at that. My eyes fluttered closed and my chin
fell.

"You need to sleep," she said.

I raised my head again and shook it to rattle myself awake.

"Tell me, Lily. These beliefs of yours . . . where do they come
from?"

The question seemed to unsettle her. She subtly wrung her
hands at her waist.

"I loved a man once. A man of faith."

"A preacher man, you mean."

"A priest, yes."

"Didn't think romance was a part of their makeup."

"It was a part of his."

I nodded. "Forbidden love, they call it."

"Yes, it was most certainly forbidden . . . and so it was also
very passionate. He opened my body and my heart to things I'd
never known before."

I scanned the room through blurred eyes. "Given your cur-
rent line of work, I take it y'all have since broke up."

"No." Her hands wrung some more. "He passed on."

"Sorry to hear that. Mind if I ask what happened?"

She stepped forward. Her eyes came up to meet mine. "Red

I looked again toward the saloon as Red Danyon shoved Lily Blanca away. The crowd parted for him as he marched toward me. He pushed me backward while tripping me up with his boot, and just like that I was flat on my back. He pressed a spur to my neck and put some weight into it.

The surrounding cowboys laughed. Everyone else gasped.

"I think it's time you died," Danyon said.

His spur pressed hard enough to cut off my wind. Panic set in. My legs quivered. My heels dug into the dirt. A full minute passed before a voice finally spoke up.

"You a sportin' man, Danyon?"

It was Duke who'd said it, but in my prone position I couldn't see him.

Above me, Danyon's head turned. "You say something, old man?" He allowed me a narrow passage of air, then pressed the spur down again.

"Way I see it," Duke said, "you're gonna make a show of killin' this fella, ya might as well put some fun into it."

Duke entered my sight line so that him and Danyon were face-to-face above me.

"I ain't sure I follow," Danyon said.

"I'm sure ya do," Duke said, wedging a fresh smoke into the corner of his mouth. He took his time getting lit. "Seems to me the good folks here would like to see if ya really got the stuff ya say you got."

Danyon went tight in the jaw. "You proposing something?"

"Might be." Duke's eyes fell to me. "Word is that Mr. Searcher here is pretty fast. I've heard the same said about you. How 'bout we find out who's faster?"

There were murmurs in the crowd.

Danyon allowed me another breath, then depressed the spur again. He turned to his brother. "You hear that, C.B.?"

"You bet I did," said Cactus Bob.

"Sounds like the old man wants to see a gunfight."

"I say we do it Texas rules," Duke went on. "One bullet each man. Let the cards fall where they may."

There was silence as Danyon scanned the crowd. "This old man right, folks? Y'all wantin' to see a gunfight?"

Only the cowboys responded. They did so with hoots and hollers.

Danyon looked down at me, then chuckled and shrugged. "Let's do it."

The spur came off my neck. I sat upright and Danyon stepped away. I was still gasping for air when Duke took hold of my ear and yanked me to my feet. My legs felt like jelly. The town was spinning around me.

Danyon moved to the center of the street. The townsfolk made for the boardwalks.

"What the hell are you doing?" I asked Duke.

"Savin' your life. He was fixin' to kill ya."

"He's still fixin' to kill me."

"Gave ya a chance, didn't I?"

Pico stepped up between us. "Just how drunk are you, Mr. Searcher?"

"Pretty damn."

Pico looked at Duke. "He can't beat him, Mr. Edwards. Not in this condition. Danyon's too fast."

"The boy speaks true, Duke. I can't beat him."

"Name's Edwards, not Duke. And you can beat him if ya believe you can."

"Problem is, I don't."

"Searcher!" Doc Watley stumbled up, a half-drunk bottle of sour mash clutched in his fist. "If you happen to take an office, I'll be in my bullet." He hiccupped and stumbled off.

Chief took the doctor's place before me. The big Comanche took off his leather necklace, from which hung a chunk of turquoise in the shape of a bear. Or maybe it was a buffalo. He placed the necklace over my head.

"For your protection," he said. "You need not worry."

"This'll prevent me taking a bullet, Chief?"

"No. But it will keep you out of hell when you die. At least it's supposed to. One never knows with these things." He sauntered off toward the boardwalk.

I asked Duke if he had any advice.

"Shoot first and don't miss," he answered. He took me by the elbow and led me into the middle of the street.

Pico fell into step with us. The boy's face was pensive. He was looking toward the western end of town.

"What is it?" I asked.

"I have an idea," he said.

He called out to ask Danyon if the proceedings could be moved down the street, where the boardinghouse windows would provide better light.

Danyon shrugged and headed that way. We followed. The crowd kept up along the boardwalks.

Pico led me under the water tower, to an open barrel brimming with murky water. Before I could ask his intentions, he took a fistful of my hair and shoved my head into the barrel. I rose up and slung back my hair.

"Sober now?" he asked.

"Not yet."

He dunked me again. When I came up the second time, I still wasn't sober, but I did feel refreshed.

"We gonna do this or what?" Danyon hollered. He assumed a stance about sixty feet up the street.

Pico led me back into the open and knelt to set my feet into position, squaring me up to Danyon.

Danyon gave the order for me to receive a gun.

Cactus Bob stepped toward me, pulled his Colt, twirled it expertly, then emptied the cylinder of all but one bullet. He slapped the revolver into my palm. The gun felt heavy and cold in my hand.

"I'm 'onna piss on your grave, you hen-shit sumbitch," he said.

He moved off, and another cowboy strapped a belt and holster to my waist. Then it was just Pico and Duke at my side.

"You're gonna make it through this," the boy said.

"Ain't sure I believe that, Pico."

"You don't have to," he said. "*I* believe it."

Pico headed off.

I set my eyes on Danyon. He'd assumed a gunfighter's stance—legs wide, arms bowed, duster draped behind the gun on his hip, fingers twitching beside the holster. Only a tight-lipped smile was visible beneath his hat brim.

"Looks like he's done this before," I said.

"There's fear in him," Duke said.

"You seein' something I ain't?"

"He's not as sure as he's letting on."

"You know the last time I shot a gun?" I said. "I was thirteen. The gun was plastic and firing a cork on a string. I never shot a real gun in my life."

Duke gave me a look of disbelief. "Hell, Searcher, didn't yer old man teach you anything?"

"My daddy only taught me one thing," I said. "But if it's all the same, I don't care to share it now."

"Then shut up and listen," Duke said. "Ya can't play catch-up in this game, so move first. Keep your arm loose. Rake up on the holster, don't go down on the handle. Don't aim and don't think. Just shoot."

He took the gun from my hand, spun the cylinder, cocked and recocked to check the action, reset the bullet in the correct chamber, then slid the weapon into the scuffed holster at my side.

"Well, anyway . . ." He ambled off toward the boardwalk.

Danyon and I were alone in the street. The flutter of torches was the only sound. I moved the wet hair off my brow, planted my feet wider, and tapped jittery fingers on my holster.

Time stretched. The sound of my heartbeat thumped in my head.

Suddenly, Danyon's fingers quit twitching.

Move first, I thought. *Goddamnit, move first!*

I was just about to when a loud wheezy hum rang out to my left. Danyon flinched. His gun fired. I jumped back and waited for the pain to register.

None did.

I opened my eyes and peered ahead. Danyon met my gaze, his pistol smoking at his side. I went for my gun, fumbled it twice, finally pulled it, closed one eye, took aim, and fired.

The bullet pinged off wood somewhere in the distance.

As my shot echoed through the valley, I heard a thud to my left. Lying facedown among the barrels beneath the water tower was Pico, a circle of red expanding beneath him, his harmonica lying in the dirt beside his hand.

I was still looking at him when the cowboys swarmed in.

And the beating started again.

I could no longer draw breath. I stopped and watched him shrink in the distance, running faster and faster.

I shielded my eyes against the blinding sun.

Beyond Sam Junior, a silhouette appeared at the edge of the horizon.

Georgia.

The sun shone through her long red hair and her short summer dress. Sam Junior met her at the horizon. They looked back at me.

I tried to call out but had no voice.

I motioned them back, but they didn't come.

Our gazes held across the vast, empty field.

Then they turned and walked hand in hand below the horizon.

I stepped forward to follow, but the ground turned soft beneath my feet. The dirt became a maw of mud. I tried to take another step but only sank farther. The earth was hungry. The ground squeezed me, swallowing my feet. My legs. My hips. My chest. I opened my mouth to scream and . . .

. . . awoke to the sound of my own cries.

Tears stung my eyes.

I tried to move, but the pain it brought was searing. My throat was hot. I tried to swallow but had no spit. I raked my tongue through my mouth and felt gaps where teeth had been. My bottom lip felt thick and heavy. My beard had grown scratchy.

When my eyes opened, the light was piercing. I'd been

stripped of my shirt, hat, boots, and socks. My pants were piss-stained and caked with dust. My skin was blistered from sun. Beneath me was hard red dirt. There was a shackle chained at my ankle.

"Rise and shine . . ."

A figure appeared above me—a black shadow against a field of white.

The voice had been deep. Familiar.

I shut my eyes against the glare and made a drinking motion with a mangled hand.

Red Danyon laughed his dull laugh.

"Later," he said. "You have nothing but time." There was more dull laughter.

The next sounds came in quick succession: The crack of a whip. The cry of a horse. The thud of running hooves. And the metallic clang of a chain pulled taut.

My body jerked, then tumbled and rolled over the hard red dirt. Eventually, the world went black and silent once more.

In the dream I saw it all happen again.

It was nighttime, and I was sitting in my truck, parked down the street from the house where my wife and boy slept.

The hours had passed slowly. The liquor had flowed steadily.

Sleep had nearly overtaken me when headlights suddenly sliced through the darkness up the street. I blinked awake and sat upright. I leaned over the steering wheel and wiped the condensation from the windshield.

The porch light outside the house caught the letters of the

Chevy's license plate as it turned into the drive: SLICK. I rubbed my watered eyes and checked my watch: 4:20. The inside of the house was dark.

I raised the whiskey from my lap and took another long pull, then set the bottle on the seat beside me. I heard the Chevy's engine die. The driver remained in the cab. I saw a lighter flare, then the glow of a cigarette ash.

I lit a Salem of my own, took two strong tokes, then flicked it away and stepped out of the truck. My legs were heavy. My balance teetered. I approached the Chevy without haste or stealth. The man saw me coming. He stepped out of the truck, rounded the hood, and we came toe-to-toe. His cigarette still burned between his lips. The brim of his Stetson was level on his head.

"What are you doing here, Bonham?"

"Waitin' on you."

"You're drunk."

"I think better when I'm drunk. Act better, too."

"Tell that to my new girlfriend and future son."

My body tightened. Adrenaline coursed through me to sobering effect.

"I thought we told you to leave," he said. "There ain't nothing for you here now."

"There's my wife and boy."

"The boy told you himself to get on out of here."

"He did," I said. "And I was listening. I just wasn't *hearing*. I'm sure as hell hearin' now."

He dropped his cigarette and crushed it under his boot. "Go on now, Bonham. Don't cause yourself any more—"

"You should know there are no more doors need fixin' in this house, anyway," I said. "That's what my boy told me."

Slick Motley said nothing.

"I'm wondering," I continued, "how it is that my son would choose those particular words when my wife had just informed me only minutes before that a stubborn door had given her that lump above the eye."

Slick Motley's tongue rolled against his cheek. He held his silence.

"Also occurs to me that my son had a swollen lip and a bruised elbow he never rightly accounted for." I peered upward into the shadow beneath the man's hat. "Did you lay rough hands on my wife and boy, you son of a bitch?"

He held my stare. His weight shifted casually. "And if I did?"

"I'm gonna make you hurt."

19.

My eyes opened with a start.

I was in a bed. Once again my vision was slow to focus. Once again everything hurt. The sheet beneath me was saturated, and I was out of breath.

I was alone in a small bedroom lit by a single lamp. Watercolor paintings hung on the walls. Beside me was a large picture window, opened slightly. White gauze curtains fluttered into the room on a warm breeze. Outside, the town of Blistered Valley was dark. The street was empty. There were only faint sounds coming out of the saloon next door. In the distance I could hear the quiet squeak of bedsprings coming out of the boardinghouse.

At the foot of the bed was a small table, on which sat a vase of wildflowers, a clay pitcher, and two tin cups. I tried to get up, but stabbing pains sent me back to the pillow with a groan.

Doc Watley rushed in.

"Take it easy, Searcher. Don't move." He checked my pulse, then pried open my eyes. His face creased with concern. "Ms. Twig!" he called. "Get me some whiskey, immediately!"

A woman in a white dress hurried in with a bottle.

"Sounds like she was escaping."

The doctor shrugged. "She had a dream. She found others who shared her dream, and together we made it a reality."

"Don't you mean a fantasy?"

He chuckled. "I suppose. We built this place up with our own hands, turning Hollywood facades into solid, three-dimensional structures, where people could live and work in harmony."

"Ain't seen much of that. Harmony, I mean."

"For a short time we lived the life we'd been searching for. Peaceful. Cut off from technology, crime, hatred. Understand, Searcher, we love our country. We just chose a better way to live in it. A simpler way."

"I seem to remember a crazy cult out in Waco saying the same thing. And those nutsos up in, what do you call it . . . Ruby Ridge."

The doctor seemed offended by the suggestions. "We were peaceful people, Mr. Searcher. We never meant harm to anyone. We just wanted to be left alone."

"Brings to mind those old hippie communes," I said.

"Yes." The doctor smiled. "In a manner of speaking, I suppose it was, only without the sex, drugs, and rock and roll. To live purer lives, we simply regressed to purer times."

"Least till the Danyons showed up . . ."

"Yes." His eyes wandered off, as though lost in the memory of it. "After discovering what we'd created here, they annexed the town and bought up even more of the surrounding land. You see, they had their own fantasies of a Utopian world built in the Old West mold. Only theirs was a fantasy world ruled by the gun."

"I see the irony."

"Yes. The place was built for cowboy movies, and that's exactly what the Danyons turned it into—their own real-life cowboy movie. And they gave themselves the starring roles."

"Anyone ever try to stand up to them. Or escape?"

"They did. And they died . . . or at the very least suffered greatly for it." The doctor went quiet. His gaze moved to the street outside the window. "But they couldn't kill us all. The cowboys needed us to sustain the town. To build and fix things. To tend to the horses, heal the sick, mend the clothes, pour the drinks . . . satisfy the sexual desires."

"You're referring to the women in the boardinghouse."

His eyes came back with intensity. "It is a service they were forced into. Danyon and his men have their way with them as they please. Three of the women took their own lives years ago, unable to cope with the abuse. Those who remained soon realized they were better off submitting than resisting, because either way the cowboys always got what they wanted."

I let this settle in on me, then asked, "And the place is totally self-contained?"

"The one notion the cowboys share with the rest of us is that the true value of this town lies in its Old West authenticity. Certainly things come up that we need, things we can't produce on our own—medicines, liquor, tobacco, food, of course. Danyon has them brought in from the outside once a month. I don't know where he receives them, but they are brought here by horse and wagon. As far as I know his funds are unlimited. He sold off most of the herd for what must have been a fortune. Any cattle he has left are mere playthings."

"How often y'all get visitors like me?"

"Hardly ever. Blistered Valley is not the kind of place one can find unless he's searching for it."

"*I* wasn't searching for it."

He smiled. "But you sure found it, didn't you? Danyon and his men ride the range every day, making sure trespassers stay clear, turning away anyone that happens onto the property by mistake. The cowboys are not the brightest of men, but they are very good at what they do. It's quite extraordinary that you and Mr. Edwards slipped in."

"Lily Blanca seems to think God had a hand in it."

"Yes. So I've heard."

"Is it true people around here think she's crazy?"

He shrugged. "Some think she is a beacon of hope. Others think she is a dreamer and a fool."

"What do you think?"

He thought hard before answering. "I want this town restored to the place it once was, Mr. Searcher. If Lily Blanca's prayers can make that possible, then I'll open my mind to anything. Until then, I shall remain a man of science." We were quiet for a moment. He pulled out his pocket watch. "It'll be morning soon. We both really must rest. I'll try and keep you here for a few more days if I can; you're certainly in no condition to work. But for now, I'll leave you. Just call if you need anything." He stood.

"Doc?"

"Yes."

"The townsfolk. Do they hate me for all the trouble I've caused? For what's happened to Pico?"

Again, he thought before he spoke "Give it time, Searcher. They'll come around. After all, you're one of us now."

When he stepped out, I thought for a while about that parting statement.

I came to the conclusion that he was dead wrong.

I wasn't one of them, nor would I ever be.

My dreams had shown me that. They'd shown me a lot, in fact. And if they'd taught me anything, it was that I couldn't put Blistered Valley behind me soon enough.

20.

I didn't wait long to make a move after the doctor left, although it hurt like holy hell to do so. After hobbling out of the bed, I moved to the closet and found the clothes I'd bought more than a week ago at the Bluebonnet Variety in Thedford. Keeping quiet so as not to alert the doctor or Ms. Twig, I stripped out of my borrowed pajamas and put on the clothes. Once dressed, I felt a little better. The movement seemed to have worked some of the pain out of my joints and muscles. With my boots in hand, I slipped out of the room through the open window.

Minutes later, I stood at the eastern end of town, staring over the darkened expanse of freedom that stretched out before me. I remained there for a time, watching the night, listening to the silence.

The corral behind me was filled to capacity. Some horses were standing. Others wallowed quietly in the dirt. I walked around the enclosure until I found Pegasus, standing just inside the fence. The wounds on his rump were still red and risen. I approached him slowly, reached through the rails, and rubbed him under the neck.

"Day he left, Mama told me he went off to do show business. The Wild West show, she said. She told me Daddy had to leave because he was gonna be a world-famous cowboy hero. I believed her."

"A world-famous cowboy? That'll be the day."

"Well, I was just a boy, and it was coming from Mama, so I believed it. But Daddy never got famous, and he didn't join any Wild West show. All he did was leave me and Mama and stay gone. And soon after he left, Mama got sick and died, and then it was just me."

Duke's face was impassive in the glow of his cigarette. "And ya never saw him again?"

"Never." I paused, swallowed. "Well, not until about two weeks ago anyway. After running out on my wife and boy and burning six months and two thousand miles in my search, I found him. In a bar. In Death Valley, California."

"And . . ."

"And he was still drunk and mean, only now he was *old*, drunk, and mean. He heard me out, acknowledged who I was, then just laughed and walked away. Last thing he said was that I should never have bothered."

Duke's cigarette flamed itself out, and he flicked it away. "How come you to go searching for him in the first place?"

I shrugged. "Looking for answers, I figure. I wanted to know why he left us. Looking at it in hindsight, maybe I felt the need to confront the sort of man I was gonna become if I didn't change my ways."

"Cowboys ride away, Searcher. Way it's always been."

"Don't make it right."

"Lots of things ain't right."

"No, they ain't," I said. "Like Mama tellin' me on her death-bed that there *were* no real heroes. No cowboy heroes, anyway, like the ones I looked up to."

"Reckon she was right?"

"I figure she said it hopin' I wouldn't ride off and wind up like Daddy. Trouble is, I wound up just like him. You asked me before if my daddy ever taught me anything. What he taught me was that I meant a whole lot less to him than he did to me . . . and now I got this awful feelin' my boy would say the same thing about me."

"Men go bad, Searcher. More often than not, I reckon. If you're looking for pity, look elsewhere."

"I ain't."

"Then if ya got a point to make, *make* it!"

"Point is, I've hurt every goddamn person that ever got close to me. And a couple of 'em are right here in Blistered Valley."

"Then maybe you best get on out of Blistered Valley. What are ya standin' around here bellyachin' for? I pulled ya a saddle. Ya got yer choice of sure-footed steeds right in this here cor-ral. And out there ya got nothin' but wide-open range as far as the eye can see. Maybe you oughtta take yer chance right now while ya got it."

"You figure?"

"It doesn't matter what *I* figure. But I'll tell ya what, Searcher. When you're good and gone, I'll open this corral and scatter these horses as best I can. Should keep those cowhands here for a while, buy you a little more time. That sound good to ya?"

We held a stare, keeping our distance. Moments passed.

"You know why I came out here?" I finally said.

"I reckon that's been established. To run."

I shook my head. "I came to see that."

I pointed toward the east, where a narrow sliver of light now stretched across the horizon.

Duke squinted into the distance. "My eyes ain't what they were last week, Searcher. You're gonna have to give me more."

"Thought I'd watch the sun rise on a new day."

Duke's eyes shifted back to me. "I reckon ya mean a *different* day."

"Hear me right, I still aim to get hell and gone from this town as soon as I can. I have things to account for back home now. My dreams showed it to me clear last night. Clearer than any dream I ever had."

"Fine."

"Also, I killed a man."

"In my experience, there's some men need killin'.'"

"They do," I said. "And the sumbitch I done in was one of 'em. But there ain't a court in the land gonna see it that way. I go home, and I'm the next one put to death. At best I'll be locked away for life. To that, I say fine. If that's how it comes to pass, I'm willing to face the music. Probably what I deserve. Only thing that matters to me is getting back to my wife and boy first. To see 'em one last time, tell 'em what I did and why I did it. To tell them I'm sorry for all the hurt I caused. What I did was—"

"What you *did* doesn't matter to me, Searcher. We've all got a past. It's what you're *gonna* do that interests me."

"Even if I told you it would require your help?"

"That depends on what you got planned."

"I'm plannin' on makin' dead every man that brought ruin to this town."

Duke took his time wetting the tip of another hand-rolled. His eyes stayed on me.

"Ain't the kind of thing you do halfway, Searcher. When the hammer drops, you can't have no second thoughts about killin'."

"I don't take killin' men lightly . . ."

"That's what worries me."

"But these men rape women," I said. "Shoot young boys. Whip horses. And they've kicked the shit out of you and me more times than I care to count. Gotta say, these things are beginning to stick in my craw."

Duke struck a match and got lit. "So what do you need from me?"

I turned my gaze toward the sleeping town. "I need you to help me remember the person I was when I still believed in the good guys. I need you to help me become that person again."

"So who was this person, Searcher?"

"He was a child, Duke. And he was a cowboy."

it. 'Bout all I can do now is promise that what you did won't have been in vain. You were right, boy. About everything. I see it all clearly now. You're a smart kid, Pico. You know, I never told you this, but I got a boy back home, 'bout the same age as you. You remind me of him a good deal. He's a good boy like you. And like you, he don't deserve the way I've treated him. Well, anyway . . . I want you to know that with Duke beside me, I aim to fight this fight to the end, even die for it if need be. I figure it's the least I can do for all you've done for me . . . hell, for all this town has done for me. You just make sure you snap out of it, you hear? You got too much fight in you not to."

There were footsteps behind me. Duke stepped in, crossed the room, and propped a hip on the windowsill. "Got a heavy look on your face," he said, sparking a fresh cigarette. "What are ya thinkin'?"

"Just hoping this boy gets to be a man," I said.

"Reckon he is already."

"Figure you're right." I brushed a tuft of hair off Pico's brow. "You know, my boy's the same age as this one."

"He a man yet?"

"Figure he is."

"Ain't an easy thing, becomin' a man. Usually happens earlier than it should."

"And usually on account of havin' to face some hard things," I said.

Duke flicked ash out the window. "When'd it happen to you?"

"When Daddy left and Mama got sick, I figure. You?"

He looked out into empty space for a time, then shook his head. "I can't remember, Searcher. You believe that?"

"I can," I said. "This might surprise you, but—"

Duke winced. He sucked a sharp breath of air through gritted teeth. His hand moved to his stomach.

"You okay?"

He could only nod. It was another minute before the pain subsided. He shook his head with a sigh. "Can't say it's good bein' old, Searcher."

"Don't figure it is," I said. "And yet we all hope to get there."

"Sure," he said. "Long as we can remember the trip."

Duke went back to smoking. I sat in the chair beside the bed and stayed quiet for a few moments, looking at Duke.

"You think about death much?" I asked.

"Never saw the point. You?"

I shook my head. "Sort of soured on the subject after watching Mama die."

"Ain't easy watching your own flesh and blood die."

The statement got me thinking on something I'd never thought of before. I looked up. "You mind sitting watch alone for a spell, Duke?"

"Name's Edwards, not Duke. Where are you going?"

"I won't be long," I said. "Just need to make a quick run to the saloon."

I left Duke to smoke and watch over Pico, and stepped one door down the boardwalk to the saloon. It was just after seven now. The sun was rising hot over the town, which was beginning to wake up. Storefronts were opening. There was the smell of bacon grease in the air.

I stepped into the saloon to find it empty, save for Chief, who sat alone in his regular seat at the end of the bar.

The saloon stank of old smoke, but it was clean. At least as clean as it could be. Glasses and bottles had been replaced on shelves. Ashtrays and spittoons had been dumped and wiped. Tilly's rolling chair was empty. Calvin, too, was nowhere in sight. I glanced up the staircase and found it dark and quiet up top. I walked down the length of the bar toward Chief. He had no glass before him.

"Feelin' better?" I asked.

"I'll live."

I reached up and took off the necklace he'd given me before the gunfight. "I ain't in hell yet, so I figure I can return this. I'm much obliged for the gesture." I handed it to him, and he replaced it around his neck. I indicated the chunk of carved turquoise hanging from the leather lace. "That's pretty," I said. "It a buffalo or a bear?"

"Wolf."

"I like it."

"It was my father's."

"He dead?"

His eyes cut over. "His throat was slit by a cowboy in a bar. A white man. I was a baby."

The Indian's speech was clipped, like movie Indians, back when movie Indians were played by guys like Rock Hudson.

"Sorry to hear that," I said. "Your daddy a good man?"

He nodded. "Important man to the tribe."

"Warrior type?"

Chief shook his head. "He brought rain."

"Quite a legacy to live up to, I figure. This town could use a good soakin'. Any of the old man's mojo fall to you?"

Chief didn't answer.

I scanned the room and asked where the boss lady was. He

pointed to a door just off the end of the bar, which until then I hadn't noticed before. I left Chief with a nod and moved toward it.

The door was open slightly, giving me a view into the space beyond. Tilly lay on a low platform bed in the corner of the room, her back pressed against the headboard. There were tears in her eyes. Calvin sat on the edge of the bed, moving her hair away from her face. I watched as he leaned over and kissed her on the mouth. There was more to the kiss than just your basic bedside manner.

I tried to back away, but the floor creaked under my feet. Calvin stood quickly. Tilly reached down and brought the bedsheet up under her chin.

"Sorry," I said. "Didn't mean to—"

"What do you want?" Tilly asked.

"I'll come back."

"For godsake, Searcher, we're decent. You got something to say, say it."

"Thought I might have a word with you, but it can wait."

"I'm too old to wait on anything." She wiped her eyes and asked Calvin to excuse us.

Calvin gave me a hard look as he brushed past me and stepped out. I moved into the room and shut the door behind me.

"Sorry," I said again. "Just didn't know you two were—"

"Now you do. Got a problem with a black man kissing a white woman?"

"I ain't like that," I answered. "Does everyone in town know?"

"It's a small town, Searcher; there are no secrets here. Sit if you want."

She grabbed a cigarette off a nearby whiskey crate and lit it. I sat on a shoeshine box in the opposite corner of the room. It was a cramped space and hot as a sweathouse. Clothes were strewn all over. Dead cigarettes littered the floor. A pair of Calvin's muddy boots stood upright at the end of the bed.

"How come you were cryin'?" I asked.

"There's a dying boy in town. It's the kind of thing that tends to dampen my spirits." She blew smoke my way.

I asked her for a cigarette, and after some hesitation she complied. I stepped over, got lit, then returned to the box.

"Why are you here, Searcher?"

"I'm wondering if you might be able to tell me a few things."

"Why should I tell you anything when nothing I say ever sinks into your thick skull?"

"How you figure?"

"I told you not to leave town, and you did. I told you to stay away from Lily, and you didn't. And because of it, you both took a beating and Pico took a bullet."

"What if I said I've had a change of heart?"

"I'd say you had no heart to change." She set an ashtray on her stomach and sent half of her cigarette lungward. "But long as you're here, go ahead and ask what you came to ask."

"I'd like to know how you came to this place."

"Why?"

"Let's just say it might be important to me later. Doc Watley tells me you came in search of the good life."

"Well, he's wrong. I came in search of a *new* life."

"What was wrong with the old one?"

"I don't want to talk about it."

"Mean a lot to me if you did."

The statement seemed to have no effect on her. I sensed that if she had legs she'd have left the room. I just stayed quiet.

After a time, she gave in. "All right, Searcher, you want it, here it is." She took a final drag on her cigarette and crushed it out with noticeable irritation. "I'd been given everything I ever wanted in life. I'd had a happy childhood. Married a good man. And after more than a dozen years of trying, I'd finally been given the one thing I'd wanted more than anything—a child."

"Don't sound like the kind of life a person would wanna run away from," I said.

"It wasn't. Until . . ." She stopped and swallowed. "Until my son was taken from me."

"Taken where? By who?"

"He died, Searcher. His name was Anthony, and I watched him die slowly of cancer at age eleven, and that's all I want to say about it."

Her words hit me hard. "Jesus, Tilly . . . I'm sorry." I gave her a moment to tamp down the emotions I could see were stirring in her. "So that's when you left?"

"I was told by everyone I knew that time would heal the pain. Life goes on, they said." She shook her head. "But life didn't go on. It couldn't. Not when everywhere I looked I saw an empty space where my boy was supposed to be. After a few years, I decided that life would only go on if I started a new one. So one day I cleared out the checking account and ceased to exist as far as anyone else knew."

"Including your husband?"

"What I needed to do couldn't be done halfway, Searcher.

I didn't even leave a note." She lit a fresh one. "Who knows, maybe I did him a favor. My grief didn't exactly enjoy company."

"So how long before you got here?"

"When I left home, I traveled the country for two years. Walking. Hitchhiking. Drifting around in no hurry. Then one day I met a man on a bus outside Diablo, Colorado. We got to talking, I told him my story, told him what I'd done to my family. He listened without judgment or comment. After hearing me out, he told me about a place called Blistered Valley. Said he thought it might interest me."

"Who was this man?"

"All I can recall of him are dark eyes, a red scarf, and the kindest smile I'd ever seen. He was handsome, and he had a gentle manner that made him easy to trust. So I put my trust in him and went in search of the place he said would be my heaven on earth. And when I saw it, I knew he was right. I bought it upon first sight."

"And everyone else? The other townsfolk, I mean. How'd they get here?"

"I met many people in my travels, made contacts, collected phone numbers."

"And they came just because you called them?"

"Most of them didn't. But clearly many of them did. I felt it was my calling to convince them to come. I can be very persuasive."

"So who were they? I mean, who were they before?"

"Just people. Like me. People wanting . . . *needing* to leave one life behind in search of another."

"Give me an example."

"Give me a name."

"Doc Watley."

"A surgeon from Edmond, Oklahoma. A divorcé with no children. When I met him, he was buried under a pending malpractice suit that was soon to end his career. I seem to remember that his drinking was involved."

"Chief . . ."

"Orphaned as a child. His mother died in childbirth, and his father was murdered. He left the reservation very young, on a quest to track down his father's killer. I met Chief in the Badlands of South Dakota, three weeks after he'd completed his search."

"Chief's an outlaw?"

"You got something against outlaws?"

I let that go.

"Marshal Pewly," I said.

"A decorated sheriff's deputy from Belpre, Kansas. He'd been caught accepting an eighty-thousand-dollar payoff from a drug ring in order to cover his own illegal gambling debt."

"Decorated, you say?"

"Once upon a time, Mr. Pewly was an extremely competent lawman. He'd only been here three months when a young filly kicked him in the head as he tried to remove a pebble from her hoof. He's not been right ever since."

"Rotten luck."

"Mr. Pewly was, and still is, a good man. He does everything within his capacity to be of service to this town."

"Calvin?"

Her lips formed a girlish smile. "A widower. He was a retired textile worker from northern Alabama, and a petty thief. I met him on a park bench in Jackson Square, New Orleans, where he'd just broken parole. We shared a bottle of wine from a bag. He told me I had great legs, and I fell in love with him on the spot."

"Legs?"

As if to avoid a reply, Tilly took a sip of water from the tin cup beside her bed. "Anyone else?" she asked.

"Yes," I said. "Tell me about Lily."

She paused to put flame to another cigarette and flung the match over her shoulder. "I met Lillian when she tried to steal my purse on an Amtrak platform in Whitefish, Montana. She was hoping to help facilitate a heroin addiction. She was pale and malnourished. I took pity and gave her fifty dollars, on the condition that she give me a number where I could reach her in the future. I told her I might be able to help her. Two months later she was here."

"So she got clean here?"

"With all of our help, yes . . . and with the help of one person in particular."

"A man."

"Yes."

"The man Danyon buried alive."

Tilly looked surprised. "She told you?"

I shrugged. "She was just fixin' to get into it when I got flung through her window. Who was he?"

Tilly scooched up on her pillow and rolled the cigarette between her yellowed fingers. "His name was Eliseo Diego. He was a pilgrim in every sense of the word. He'd been a free-spirited adventurer, who at eighteen had gotten stranded in a snowstorm while hiking alone somewhere out west. Sick with frostbite and delirium, he made the typical survival deal with God."

"And what happened?"

"They both made good. God saved Diego. Diego dedicated his life to spreading the Good Word."

"Where'd you run into him?"

"At a breakfast counter in Lincoln, Nebraska. I found him sitting alone before a Denver omelet and the book of Leviticus. He was handsome, with dark skin and a pleasant smile. We shared our stories, and I liked him immediately. He had an idealism I found infectious. Six months later, I called him, and he came right away. Seems he felt it was his calling to serve as the spiritual backbone of this town. It was he who built the church atop the southern plateau."

"And him and Lily?"

"They arrived within weeks of each other and fell in love instantly . . . as I knew they would."

"So it was a setup?"

"Yes. Diego showed Lily a way of life she'd never known. For the first time in her life she was happy."

"When'd it go wrong?"

"When it all went wrong, Searcher . . . when the cowboys arrived. The day they took over, we lost everything, including the freedom to leave at will. Blistered Valley became a prison from which no escape was possible. And Red Danyon became obsessed with Lily the moment he saw her."

"Not hard to do."

"For their own safety, Diego and Lily kept their relationship a secret."

"Until?"

When Tilly didn't respond, I finished for her.

"Until Lily got pregnant . . . right?"

"Now it's your turn, Searcher. How is it that *you* wound up here . . . and on the same day as an old man whom you claim to be a stranger to you?"

In the time it took me to burn through two cigarettes, I told her my story from the very beginning: The search for my father. My return home to Welshland. The killing of Slick Motley, and my run from the law. I also told her about the plane crash and the episode with the silver box, leaving out only one detail—Duke's true identity. For the moment, I chose to keep that between me and Lily and Pico. I sensed that Tilly hadn't fully swallowed the part about the old man's rise from a frozen grave, but she neither questioned it nor expressed any disbelief. She just stayed quiet, thoughtfully rolling her cigarette between her fingers.

"So, tell me," she said. "You claim to have had a change of heart. What exactly does that mean?"

"Can't rightly say I've got it figured out yet. All I know is I got a wife and boy back home who deserve an apology and explanation, but I can't get there because I'm trapped here. I also know that there are some people in this town I've grown fond of, and they're hurtin'. One of them is a sick boy who needs proper medical treatment, and he needs it quick. Put it all together, and I figure there's some cowboys around here that need killin'."

She peered at me through the smoky haze between us. "You're serious?"

"As stomach cancer."

"Why would you help us?"

I thought hard before answering. "You've been talkin' a lot about folks answering calls. Maybe this is my higher calling."

"You're just one man, Searcher. The cowboys are many."

"I have help."

"Who?"

"Mr. Edwards."

"He's a sick old man."

"That he is. But I figure that sick old man is answering a higher calling of his own. He did fall from the heavens, after all. Technically speaking, anyway."

Tilly considered it.

"Are you trying to tell me that sick old man is the answer to Lily's crazy prayers?"

"No," I said. "*I'm* the answer to Lily's crazy prayers. That sick old man is the answer to mine."

22.

Pico was no longer the only one laid up in Doc Watley's examination room when I returned.

I walked in to find Duke lying prone on the floor, Ms. Twig kneeling beside him, fanning his sweaty bald head with a dust-pan. Duke's blackened toes were curled, and he was groaning in pain.

I was still standing unnoticed at the door when Doc Watley stepped up behind me, took hold of my elbow, and pulled me quietly around the corner into his office.

"What happened?" I asked.

"Minutes after you left, he started complaining again about the pains in his abdomen. They seem to be getting worse. He was describing them to me when a stabbing pain suddenly buckled his legs right out from under him."

"Hell . . ."

"Do you know anything about that man's health that you haven't told me, Searcher? I get a sense you two have a history. I'm afraid no one believes it just a coincidence you two hap-pened to arrive in town on the same day."

The question caught me off guard. I just shrugged and shook my head.

"He's a very sick man," the doctor said. "Sicker than he's been letting on, I'm afraid."

I cleared my throat. "I'm just pulling at straws, Doc, but my guess is belly cancer. But of course, you're the expert."

"You may be more right than you know. I would have thought it just an ulcer if not for the scar over his stomach. He's had professional treatment at some stage; I can see it in the stitching."

"Let's say for argument's sake it is belly cancer, Doc. If you had to take a guess, what's he looking at? Weeks?"

"Days."

"Shit." But it made sense. After all, the cancer had already killed Duke once. Thirty years on ice wouldn't have made him any less sick. "I wonder, Doc, if there's any chance—"

"Get me whiskey!"

It was Duke's voice, calling from the other room. Another groan followed the request.

Doc Watley grabbed a bottle off his desktop, and we rushed back into the examination room. With Ms. Twig's assistance, the doctor funneled a sizable slug of sour mash down Duke's throat. Duke coughed and sputtered as the liquor went down, but its effect was immediate. His toes slowly uncurled. He sat upright.

"Smoke," he said.

I looked at the doctor. The doctor shrugged. I gave Duke a hand-rolled and lit it. He struggled on the first few inhalations, but the cigarette brought color to his cheeks. It took all three of us to lift the big man back to his feet.

When he found his balance, he belted another pull of sour mash, then nodded. "Come on, Searcher, we got work to do."

We stepped out under a sweltering midmorning sun.

"So what do we do first?" I asked.

"Eat," he said. "I'm hankerin' for a T-bone."

I looked him up and down, taking in his calf-length pants, tattered peasant shirt, and bare feet. "Duke, I'm thinkin' these clothes don't quite fit your image."

"Why do you keep calling me Duke?"

"Sorry, force of habit. Just suits you, I figure. You mind?"

"Reckon not. Come to think of it, I kind of like it." He eyed me as I had done him. "Ya wanna be a cowboy, Searcher, you could stand for some new clothes yourself. Come on, let's go get into character."

There was some bustle on the street now. Meandering through horse and foot traffic, we crossed the road and ducked into the general store. The store was dark and smelled of dust. The shelves were jammed with everything from powdered toothpaste and hair oil to lye soap and snuff tins.

Duke's size limited his clothing options, but he managed to find a pair of work pants that were only a couple inches short, and a pearl-snap shirt that fit all right once he rolled up the sleeves. He also picked out a blue bandanna, which he knotted loosely at his neck.

The shopkeeper was a hospitable man who introduced himself as Tom Bob Finkle. Mr. Finkle presented Duke with the only pair of size 14 boots he had. They were tall in the stock and had a nice riding heel, and proved to be a good fit. Sliding into the boots brought out the first genuine smile I'd seen on Duke's face since we'd met.

We both rejected a half-dozen hat choices before we found keepers. I went for a camel-brown felt with a narrow brim folded low in the front and high on the sides. Duke settled on a cavalry-style hat with a wide brim and a tall crown. Both hats were bent-up hand-me-downs, but the look was right and the fit was good.

I told Duke I wanted spurs.

"Spurs?"

"Indulge me."

We each got a pair. Duke strapped mine on for me, then put on his own.

I stomped my feet. The spurs were rusty and made no sound.

"They don't jangle," I said.

"Jangle?"

"I want 'em to jangle."

"Ya get to usin' 'em, Searcher, they'll jangle." He smiled. "It's called earnin' your spurs."

I asked Duke how they looked. He didn't answer. He just told me not to squat with them on.

I told Mr. Finkle to put the charges on Tilly's tab. He shrugged, licked the tip of his pencil, and made marks on a notepad. At the counter we stocked up on tobacco, rolling paper, and matches. Duke pulled a candy cane from a jelly jar and chomped the whole thing down while we stood there.

On our way out, we checked our reflection in the shop window.

Drawn and sickly, Duke was still an unrecognizable shadow of the screen legend he'd once been . . . but he did look the part.

I looked every bit the scrawny drywall man playing dress-up.

I didn't care.

23.

We stepped into the café minutes later.

Sandwiched between the barbershop and the boardinghouse on the south side of the street, there weren't a lot of frills to the place. It was crowded, airless, and hot. The head of a boar hog was the only wall decoration. There were a few townspeople scattered around the room, but the tables were mostly full of cowboys soaking up last night's drunk with grease and batter.

All eyes turned our way as me and Duke crossed the room and took our seats at the only empty table. A few cowboys grinned and giggled as we went past. We paid them no mind, and soon they went back to slugging coffee and sopping up egg yolk with hunks of cornbread.

The waitress came over, and we both ordered steak and eggs with coffee. She went off, and we lit fresh cigarettes. I got to thinking.

"Can I ask you something, Duke? That Winchester out in the desert . . . I tried to pull it out of the ground, but it wouldn't budge. Damn thing was dug in like it was stuck in cement."

There was more laughter. I started to stand, but Duke placed a firm hand on my arm.

"We got no trouble here, Danyon," Duke said.

"'Fraid you do, old man. Like I said, you boys are at our table."

"Find another," Duke said.

The Danyons shared a glance, then Cactus Bob stepped in and took hold of the table, like he aimed to flip it.

"I wouldn't," I said.

Cactus Bob's eyes shifted my way. Our faces were inches apart. "Oh yeah," he said. "Why's 'at?"

I indicated Duke with a nod. "'Cause I've seen what happens when someone fucks with this man's T-bone."

I'd spoken true. Lee Marvin had ruined Duke's steak in *The Man Who Shot Liberty Valance*. I figured if Duke could wilt Lee Marvin with just a few words and a stern look, there was no telling what he might do to Cactus Bob's dumb ass.

But then in the movie Woody Strode had been standing at the kitchen door, rifle in hand, covering Duke's back. All that stood at the kitchen door now was our waitress holding Cactus Bob's beans.

Cactus Bob laughed, deepened his leg bend, and then tipped the table. Eggs flew. Dishes shattered. Our steaks hit the floor with a splat.

Then the only sound in the room was the creak of bones as Duke squared up to Cactus Bob.

"I seem to remember askin' ya nice to let us be," Duke said.

"That's right," said Cactus Bob. "But I didn't, did I?"

"How come they to call you Cactus Bob?" asked Duke.

"'Cause I'm a prickly fucker," answered Cactus Bob.

More laughter.

"Careful, brother," Red Danyon said, as he rolled a fresh cigar over a struck match. "Looks like you might have pissed the old buzzard off."

"Just might have," Cactus Bob said with a grin. He took another step toward Duke. "You gonna do somethin' 'bout it, old man?"

Duke widened his stance. His hands went to his hips. "What say I answer that question outside? Just you and me."

With a thumb, Cactus Bob raked the chaw out of his cheek and flicked it down onto Duke's new boots. "Why bother to step outside, old-timer? What say we do it right here?"

Cactus Bob drew back a fist but paused at the sound of a cocking gun.

His eyes opened wide. He peered down slowly as I pressed the barrel of his own gun against his balls.

"You're right," I said to Duke. "Works better when you drag your hand up the holster."

Cactus Bob's mistake had been crouching down so close to me. I'd pulled his gun just as he'd sprung to upend the table, so fast not a man in the room had seen it.

Red Danyon's hands moved to his pistols.

"You best let go of them Colts," I said. "'Less you want to accessorize your outfit with chunks of your brother's nuts."

Danyon's features went tight. "How did you—"

"I'm fast, that's how." I sprung to my feet and placed the gun at the back of Cactus Bob's head.

Chairs scooted back in all directions. Every gun in the room was pulled and cocked and aimed my way.

"No!" said Cactus Bob, the barrel of my gun pressed hard to

his skull. "Don't none a y'all do nothin'!" Then to his brother, "Goddamnit, Red, do somethin'!"

"Ya can start by telling your men to drop the guns," Duke said to Danyon.

Danyon scanned the room. He told his men to drop their guns. The floor shook under the clatter of heavy steel.

"You, too," Duke instructed Danyon. "Slowly."

Danyon, looking fit to blow, did as he'd been told.

"I reckon you can take it from here, Mr. Searcher," Duke said.

I looked at him.

He nodded.

I nodded back. "Okay then. It's like this. Here's what's gonna happen . . ." Trouble was, I had no idea what was going to happen. My mouth had gone dry. Panic set in quick.

Duke seemed to pick up on it. "We need horses," he said.

"That's right, we need horses," I said.

I looked at our waitress, who was still standing wide-eyed and slack-jawed at the kitchen door with Cactus Bob's beans.

"What's your name, darlin'?" I asked.

"Cinnamon Morehouse."

"Good name," I said. "Ain't that a good name?"

"Reckon it is," Duke said.

"Ms. Morehouse, I wonder if I could trouble you to step out and rustle up a couple good horses for me and Mr. Edwards here."

Cinnamon Morehouse hesitated some, but eventually she set down the bean plate and went out the front door.

All eyes swung back my way.

I figured it was time to stall. I cleared my throat and stood up straight to look taller. In my lowest possible register, I said, "All right all you shit kickers, listen up. Y'all should know that the only reason I wound up in this dustbin is 'cause I lost the goddamn plot last week and killed this big bastard of a cowboy on my own wife's front lawn. I was out of my skull pissed off, and I gutted the son of a bitch like a brook trout. And I'm glad I done it, too, because he was a worthless shit ass just like this one." I whacked Cactus Bob in the head with the butt of the pistol. "Hope that gives you peckerwoods some idea of just how fucked up and unpredictable I am."

I cut my eyes over to the door, saw no sign of Cinnamon Morehouse.

I stalled some more. "And another thing, you heifer-lovin' sons of bitches . . . I'm sober now. And when I'm sober, I get rankled easy. So there's no telling the shit I'm liable to pull." To drive home the point, I clocked Cactus Bob again. Then I looked back at the door. Still no Cinnamon Morehouse. "And not only that," I droned on, "but there was this one time at the Tilt 'N Bowl outside Tulsa—"

The front door clanged. I turned. Instead of Cinnamon Morehouse, I found Denver Mack and Spittoon Miller. Their mouths fell open when they took in the situation. A rope of drool spilled off Spittoon Miller's lip.

"Speaking of heifer lovers . . ." I said. "Howdy, boys. Toss your guns and join the party."

Denver Mack and Spittoon Miller looked to Red Danyon. At his nod, the men dropped their weapons.

Before I could return to the Tulsa story, the door clanged again. Cinnamon Morehouse stepped in, looked at me, and raised a thumb.

Bob's temple, Duke wedged his reins between his teeth, then leaned out, and with his free hand took hold of my horse's reins. He yanked hard on both sets of reins, and the horses kicked dust and skidded to a stop.

"Get off!"

I didn't know if Duke was talking to me or Cactus Bob, but we both tumbled from our respective saddles. Shots kept coming from the boardinghouse. Bullets thudded the dirt all around us.

I made it to my feet, only to find myself disoriented in the dust.

"What are ya waitin' for, Searcher, get in here!"

I turned and sprinted blindly, following the sound of Duke's voice. I tripped on my own spur and tumbled onto the boardwalk. From there I continued on in a mad crawl.

Suddenly, I was indoors.

A door slammed.

The shooting outside ceased.

There was a beat of quiet.

Then a cheery voice said, "Welcome, men!"

24.

Taking us both by the collar, Duke jerked me and Cactus Bob to our feet.

Duke told me to draw my gun. We were standing in the main room of the jailhouse looking at Marshal Pewly, who stood behind his desk wearing a broad smile.

"Mr. Searcher! Mr. Edwards! Cactus Bob! What brings y'all—"

Duke extended his gun.

The marshal's hands shot up.

"Head into that cell room, open the cage, and whistle when you're done," Duke ordered the marshal.

"Yes sir, Mr. Edwards!" Pewly licked a clump of oatmeal off his bottom lip. "Only . . ."

"Only what?"

"I can't whistle."

"Clap then."

Pewly hustled into the cell room. Within seconds I heard the rattle of keys, the turn of a lock, and the clap of hands.

While Duke moved to cover the front window, I nudged Cactus Bob into the next room. Marshal Pewly yielded way for the hostage to enter the cell. I told Cactus Bob to get comfortable. He cussed me. I heard the rumble of hoofbeats on the street outside.

"Duke?"

"It's all right," Duke answered. "They're just kicking up dust, making a show. Looks like they all aim to mount up down at the livery."

Worry crept over Marshal Pewly's face. We shared a look. He drew his toy cap gun.

Cactus Bob laughed as he took a seat on the cot.

"Somethin' funny?" I asked.

"All three a you sumbitches are good as dead."

I asked Marshal Pewly if he'd be kind enough to cuff Cactus Bob's hands and ankles.

Pewly paled. "Cuff him?"

"Don't worry," I said. "He won't try nothin'."

I extended the Colt through the bars and set my aim on Cactus Bob's face.

Pewly took down the two sets of manacles hanging on the wall behind him. He stepped into the cell, cuffed Cactus Bob's hands behind his waist, then cuffed his ankles. When it was done Cactus Bob spat on my boots and called me a fuckstump.

I held my calm.

"Marshal Pewly?" I said. "I wonder if you might shove one of your socks into the prisoner's mouth and secure it with that bandanna he's wearing."

"Yes, sir, Mr. Searcher." Pewly had it done in less than a minute. Cactus Bob was left mumbling his curses through a mouthful of foot sweat.

I told the marshal to cover his ears, and he obeyed. I stepped up to the bars and asked Cactus Bob if he knew that the marshal wasn't right in the head.

Cactus Bob barked something through the sock.

I nodded. "That's what I thought." I motioned for Pewly to uncover his ears, then held out my loaded pistol. "Marshal, if you'd watch this man for a spell, I'd sure appreciate it. Should he give you any trouble, shoot him."

"Yes, sir, Mr. Searcher."

I relieved Marshal Pewly of his cap 'n' ball Colt. He took my real pistol in greedy hands and slipped it into his holster. I left him with a confident slap on the back, then moved to join Duke in the front room.

"Stay away from the window," Duke said.

I stayed close to the wall and crouched low, out of the line of fire. I asked Duke what was happening outside.

Pistols cocked, he rose to a kneeling position below the window and peered out. "Most of 'em are mounted."

The cowboys were running their steeds up and down the street, hooting and hollering and firing their Colts into the air. Some were running circles around the water well, just outside the jailhouse.

Duke sat back down under the window, his back pressed to the wall. A smile curved one side of his mouth. "I know we aimed to stir some dust in this town, Searcher, but I didn't know ya had it in ya to do what you did."

"Maybe I'm cut out for this kind of work after all."

"Your skill in the saddle could use some work." He glanced toward the back room. "Ya reckon the half-wit back there's good to stand a post?"

"I gave him my gun."

Duke looked at me with concern.

I shrugged. "Tilly told me Pewly was a damn good lawman back when he had all his marbles. I got a feeling he's still got it in him."

"Hope yer right," Duke said. "Still, we're gonna need that gun back."

"It's got five in the cylinder. Yours?"

Duke checked his guns, then reached behind his waist and counted the bullets on his belt. "Six and five in the Colts. Twelve on the belt."

"That ain't gonna go far."

"Not if we're plannin' on—"

A gun fired at close range. The window above Duke's head fell in a cascade of broken shards. He shook his hat free of glass, then fired a blind shot over each shoulder. Outside, I heard the shooter scurry off.

"Make that five and four in my guns," Duke said.

Outside, riders continued to thunder past in both directions. Guns blazed. More and more bullets whizzed and pinged over our heads, pocking the jailhouse walls.

"What the hell are they doing?" I asked.

"Playing with us," Duke said. "Hopin' to draw our fire."

I rose just high enough to get a glimpse outside, and when I did a bullet whooshed past my ear. I dropped back down. Another bullet blew the potted cactus plant off Pewly's desk.

"We ain't gonna last long like this," I said.

"Reckon you're right," Duke said. "They need a nudge."

Duke peered out the window and nearly lost his head for it. Three quick shots from outside brought him hunkering back down.

"Who's that one always drippin' chaw down his chin?"

"Spittoon Miller," I said.

Duke recocked, rose up, fired twice, and sat back down. "He's dead now."

"Hell, Duke . . ."

"What?"

"You just up and killed him."

"Ya sorry about it?"

"Just not used to it."

"Best you get used to it. Now they know we mean business."

"Goddamn you, sumbitches!" called a voice from outside. "I'm gonna kill the both of you!"

This from Denver Mack. I recognized the high, nasally pitch. I figured he'd just seen what Duke had done to his buddy.

"Searcher! Edwards!" It was Red Danyon calling now. "Y'all hearin' me?"

I looked at Duke. Duke nodded for me to answer.

"We're hearin' you," I said.

"You killed one of my men."

"We know that," I said. "And your brother's next, you and your men don't get your asses out of town this minute."

"You threatenin' me, Searcher?"

"I am. Now get on out, or it's your ass."

"The hell it is," Danyon said. "I'm gonna scalp both you fuckers, then watch your skulls bleed out."

"I must not be speakin' clear," I said. Talking loud enough for Danyon to hear, I yelled for Marshal Pewly to shoot Cactus Bob in the toe.

Marshal Pewly shot Cactus Bob in the toe.

Behind me Cactus Bob laughed through Marshal Pewly's sock.

The marshal, who sat in a chair outside the cell, offered me an encouraging thumbs-up and a smile.

I turned back to Duke. "But it *was* better, right?"

He put flame to another hand-rolled and shook his head. "Ya still gotta relax that grip. It's a gun, Searcher, not a sledge-hammer. No need to white-knuckle it. Quit closin' that eye, too, you're gonna need 'em both. And for the last time, don't lock your elbow."

"What about aimin'?"

"What about it?"

"How do I?"

"Ya don't. Aimin's thinkin'. Thinkin'll only get ya killed. It's more about feelin'."

"Can I have a practice shot?"

"Ain't got the bullets for that."

"Just one."

He relented. "One." He slid a pistol to me across the floor and pointed to the back wall. "Hit Texas."

The state map hung on the wall to my right, about twelve feet away. I picked up the gun, widened my stance, took a breath, relaxed my limbs, extended the weapon, cocked, and fired.

Had it been a national map, I'd have hit somewhere near Vermont.

"You shoot about like you ride horses, Searcher. Now ya see where thinkin'll get ya. Don't do it."

"Easier said than done."

"Everything's easier said than done. Get over here."

I crawled to join him beneath the window, avoiding the broken glass scattered about the floor. Duke raised his head and looked outside. A bullet pinged the wood in front of his nose, and he came back down.

"Ya know the cowhand I shot?" Duke said.

"Spittoon Miller."

"They left him where he fell, right next to the water well out there."

"So . . ."

"So they also left his guns on him. You run, I'll cover ya. When ya get to the well, keep low, 'less ya wanna lose your head. I'll draw their fire, hopefully give ya a look at 'em. When your gun empties, take the Colts off the dead man."

He called for the marshal to toss me the gun I'd lent him.

I caught it, then cocked it with a thumb that was slick with nervous sweat.

Duke looked at me and nodded. "Ya run like hell, you'll be all right. Whatever ya do, don't stop till ya get there. Go."

"First, I think I might oughtta—"

"Go!"

Aided by Duke's double-fisted yank on my shirt, I launched upward from the floor and dove headlong out the window. I somersaulted when I hit the boardwalk, then rolled onto my feet and ran. Duke's pistols blazed cover fire from behind.

Rifle shots from above kicked dust at my feet. Still ten feet shy of the well, I dove again, belly-skidded, then crawled the rest of the way. I pressed my back against the well wall and looked back toward the jailhouse. Duke had already hunkered back below the window ledge under a barrage of gunfire.

He'd been right. The shooters were at rooftop perches on opposite ends of town. Both were alternating their aim between the jailhouse window and the stones above my head. Rock fragments rained down on me.

I felt warmth at the seat of my pants, and realized that I was sitting in a pool of Spittoon Miller's blood. Beside me, the dead cowboy was already drawing flies.

"Aim west, I'll shoot east," Duke hollered. "Count of three, ready?"

Before I could answer, Duke counted off and came up firing.

I followed, exposing only my head and shooting arm above the wall. My eyes found a lanky silhouette atop the boarding-house. My thumb pulled the hammer, and my finger tickled the trigger. Bullets whizzed at my ears like buzzing gnats. Before I knew it, my load was empty, and I was hunkered down again behind the wall.

Duke, too, had ducked out of sight . . . or been shot.

I called out to him.

"Reload!" came his reply.

I tossed away the gun I'd come out with and reached for the one holstered on Spittoon Miller's right hip. The Colt was long-barreled, with a pearl handle. I checked its cylinder, found a full load, and cocked it.

"Count off, Duke!"

He did. We came up blazing again. Like before, we emptied our loads quick and ducked back down. Rifle fire kept coming from both directions. I reached for Spittoon Miller's other pistol, checked the cylinder, and found only two bullets. His gun belt was empty.

Shouting over the volley of flying lead, I relayed this discovery to Duke.

"Two bullets . . . two men," he hollered back.

I cussed.

I wiped sweat from my eyes. The rifle fire kept coming like a storm. I felt a flick on my right boot, and looked down to see that a corner of my heel had been shot off. I curled my legs up against my chest.

Another bullet chipped the wall right above my head.

I caught something gleaming in the corner of my eye. Spittoon Miller's belt buckle, catching the sun. It was oval in shape and smooth on the face.

Keeping low, I reached down and unsnapped the buckle from the belt. Holding it out from my chest, I tilted it upward and eastward. In the reflection I had a blurred but decipherable image of the shooter crouched behind a raised portion of the livery stable roof, under a skillion overhang.

I raised my left arm, exposing it above the well wall. In the reflection, I saw the shooter respond, stepping away from his cover just long enough to get off a shot. I lowered my arm, waited a beat, then repeated the action. Again, the shooter took a half step away from his cover to shoot. His shot brushed the hair on my arm.

Once again, I raised my arm to draw fire. When I heard the first shot, I quickly rolled away, came up into a kneeling position, and pulled the trigger. I was already back under cover when I heard the dull thud of the gunman's body hitting dirt at the end of the street.

"Heard that," said an unseen Duke from the jailhouse.

eyes and the sweat on his brow that his gut was hurting him bad.

After I'd killed the riflemen, it was some time before anyone felt safe to walk the street again. Me and Duke had been the first to step out into the open. We walked the length of the town twice, guns cocked at our sides, eyes peeled, checking windows and rooftops for more gunmen. The town had gone eerily quiet. We saw no sign of any more of Danyon's men.

When the townsfolk finally began to emerge from the buildings, I sensed their fear immediately. I also sensed their anger. I figured a lot of it had to do with the death of Mr. Finkle. Some probably thought that me and Duke were partly to blame for that. They might have been right. Mr. Finkle's death still wasn't sitting right with me. For that matter, neither was the death of the two cowboys I'd killed.

It had been almost an hour since the guns had gone silent, but tempers had yet to simmer in the saloon.

"What if we just turned these two over to Danyon?" asked a gaunt man with a pinched face, from over near the fireplace. "Maybe then he'd go easier on us."

"Worth a thought," someone said. "I'd like to slap 'em both around a little first, though."

"Hear, hear!"

"Second that!"

"I got dibs on the little fella!"

This line of discussion went on for a while, until Duke drew his Colt and fired off a round.

Women screamed. So did a few men. Then a hush fell over the room.

I looked up, ears ringing, to find that Duke had shot the

snout off Carne Muerto, the steer mounted above the bar. The snout had landed behind the bar at the foot of Tilly's rolling chair.

"Anyone else like to speak his mind?" Duke asked, his Colt still breathing smoke.

"You're crazy," said a jowly man to our right. "Plumb crazy."

Duke rounded and drove a fist into the man's jaw, knocking him cold. "Anyone else?"

No one spoke then.

Duke slowly took in the room, scanning faces. "Danyon said he'd be back at sundown. Which means we're wastin' time. Isn't that right, Mr. Searcher?"

"Figure it is," I said.

"So it's time to quit bellyachin' and start plannin'," Duke said.

"We already got a plan, old man," said a townsman seated at one of the tables behind us. "We're gonna turn Cactus Bob loose."

Duke's eyes narrowed. "You and how many others?"

The man's hands coiled into fists, like he was thinking about doing something with them, but hadn't fully committed to it. He was mid-forties and had cracked skin. The muscles in his arms looked chiseled by hard work.

"You can't stop us all, old man," he said to Duke.

Duke grinned. "Fella could mistake you for a man with grit, mister." He asked the man his name and business.

"Cotton Chatwick. Blacksmith."

"Well, Mr. Chatwick . . ." Duke took another sip of whiskey, then drew his Colt again and slid it down the length of the bar, shattering glasses. "Ya care to take a turn with me right now?"

The question seemed to suck the air out of the room. The atmosphere grew thick. Mr. Chatwick's right eye twitched. Otherwise, he held still.

"Didn't reckon ya did," Duke said. "Perhaps ya'd like a turn with Mr. Searcher, here."

Mr. Chatwick looked my way. He was a bigger man than me. I kept my expression hard. Seconds passed. At last, Mr. Chatwick looked off.

Duke asked if anyone else wanted to take a turn with either of us. No one came forward.

"They're pretty good with their mouths, aren't they, Mr. Searcher?" Duke said.

"Figure they are."

"Seems not a one of 'em wants to back it up with a fist."

"Don't look like it."

Nervous glances were exchanged across the room.

Duke belted the last of his whiskey and tipped his glass on the bar. His feet staggered. His hands went to his hips. His eyes went back to Mr. Chatwick. "What say we get down to business, then."

Mr. Chatwick took a long drink of beer, as if to calm himself. "Okay. Let's get down to business. I'm sure we'd all love to hear *your* plan."

"All right then, I'll tell ya," Duke said. "When Danyon comes back, we're gonna ransom his brother for every saddled horse in the town. All you folks'll mount up and head out first, taking Danyon's brother with ya. You'll keep him shackled and under gun at all times. Searcher and I will stay behind."

"Why?" asked Mr. Chatwick. "To get killed?"

"To buy time," Duke said. "I reckon two hours' head start

should be enough to put ya in the clear. Before ya head out, we'll make sure Danyon knows that if me and Searcher haven't caught up with you in three hours' time, his brother dies. That's how it's gonna go." He turned to me. "Unless you have anything to add, Mr. Searcher."

I didn't.

Mr. Chatwick rubbed at his whiskers, thinking. "And when . . . or *if* you and Mr. Searcher do catch up with us? What then?"

"We dump Danyon's brother in the desert with a full canteen and a plug of jerky. Then we all go our separate ways."

Tilly shook her head. "Danyon's not gonna give up those horses, old man. He's gonna kill us off one by one until we let his brother go."

Duke didn't take kindly to being argued with. His next words were spoken low, through gritted teeth.

"If Danyon wanted to kill you, woman, he'd have done it already. He needs you people."

"Not all of us," said Mr. Chatwick. "Danyon wouldn't hesitate to kill a good many of us if it meant getting his brother back. Don't you get it, old man? We have no choice but to free Cactus Bob."

"You must not be hearin' me right," Duke said. "I just gave ya another choice. It's the best option you're gonna get. Now you people either run from these cowhands as fast as you can or—"

"He's right, Duke." I'd said it before I could even think not to. It was like the words had left my mouth beyond my control. But they were out there, and I'd pulled the focus of every eye in the room, including Duke's.

"Care to repeat that, Mr. Searcher?" Duke asked.

The words didn't come out so easy the second time, saying them under Duke's glare.

"Mr. Searcher?" said Mr. Chatwick. He alternated glances between me and Duke. "You have something to add?"

The room was quiet. I took a breath and swallowed. Then I looked Duke in the eye and told him he was wrong.

Smoke seeped through Duke's clenched teeth.

"Danyon ain't gonna deal," I said. "He ain't gonna surrender his horses . . . which means we ain't gonna run."

"Then what *are* we gonna do?" Mr. Chatwick asked.

"We're going to fight."

Lily Blanca had said the words before I could.

All heads turned her way. She was standing midway down the staircase. A white dress with yellow flowers had replaced her whore clothes. She wore no makeup or jewelry. The sight of her stole my breath again.

We shared a nod.

"Lily's right," I said.

"We're fighting nothing," said Mr. Chatwick. "You're a fool, Lily. With foolish hope."

"There's nothing foolish about hope," Lily said.

"I remember Father Diego telling us the same thing twelve years ago," said Mr. Chatwick. "Look where hope got him."

Lily offered no reaction to the mention of Diego's name.

"These men can help us," she said, indicating me and Duke. "They owe us nothing. Nor do they have anything to gain by fighting for us. The least we can do is join them and fight for ourselves. It's a fight worth dying for, if need be."

"Easy for you to say," said Tilly.

"Yes, it is," Lily said. "My soul is ready. Can you say the same?"

Tilly blew cigarette smoke and looked away.

"But how can we stand up to those cowboys?" asked an elderly woman to my left. "We aren't fighters. And we have nothing to fight with. No guns."

"We'll take guns off dead cowboys," I said. "We've done it once; we'll do it again."

The old woman held my stare. "You seem to have it all figured out, Mr. Searcher."

"Yes, ma'am," I said. "I figure I do. And if you'll hear me out, you might just come around to—"

"I'll fight."

It was one of the cooks from the café who'd spoken. He stood at the front of the saloon, just inside the batwing doors.

Mr. Chatwick rose out of his chair. "Checker Dobson, are you crazy?"

Checker Dobson's eyes were still on me. "I'll fight," he said again.

Then another voice echoed the statement. I turned to find Chief stepping forward. He gave me a nod.

More nods followed. Others spoke up to volunteer their services. The room began to bustle with movement.

I suddenly realized that Duke was no longer at my side.

I looked around and found him standing at the far end of the bar, peering sideways at me. He lit a cigarette between cupped hands and let his mouth curl up on one side to let smoke escape. It almost looked like a smile. After a few beats he pounded the bar with his empty glass, called for quiet, and got it. "All right then, Mr. Searcher, the floor's yours," he said. "Tell us all how it's gonna go down."

I did.

I told the townsfolk again that there'd be no dealing with Danyon.

I said there'd be no fleeing on horseback.

And I told them that come sundown, Danyon was going to ride into town to find his brother already hung.

27.

The hours passed quick then, the way hours do when there's a lot of work to be done and not enough time to do it in.

The first thing me and Duke did was take stock of our munitions. The picture wasn't a good one. We'd taken five Colts off the cowboys, but had only seven rounds among them. We sent men up to the roofs of the boardinghouse and the livery stable to see what they could find, other than the cowboys I'd killed. Each man had returned with a Marlin Model rifle in hand.

As expected, they'd reported a large number of spent shell casings scattered around the dead cowboys, but me and Duke had nearly taken them for all the ammo they had. Between the two gunmen, there were only nine rifle rounds left. I'd already been told that the cowboys stashed their replacement ammo somewhere outside of town. Bottom line, we'd be fighting twenty-seven well-armed men with sixteen bullets spread out between seven guns.

I asked the two men who'd returned with the rifles their names.

"Eli Blanton," answered one of the men. He was maybe sixty,

watched him for a few moments. He didn't seem to draw a breath that didn't hurt.

Chief sauntered up from behind me, wet with sweat and even redder in the face than usual. He'd been cutting wood under the water tower for more than an hour. Sawdust was caked in the sweat on his arms.

"Done down there," he said.

"We good?"

"We're good. What's next?"

I dropped my cigarette and crushed it. "I need the assistance of a woman out here, Chief. Mind fetching her for me?"

"Depends on the woman," he said.

I told him.

He smiled like I was joking. When he saw that I wasn't, his smile vanished. "She ain't gonna come voluntarily," he said.

"Figure she won't. You're gonna have to charm her."

"Can't charm a lady don't wanna be charmed."

"Well then, force yourself on her if you have to. But we need her."

He took a deep breath and looked hard into my eyes. "I'll do my best."

"All I can ask."

He moved off. As he went, I watched him rip open the snaps of his denim shirt and shrug out of it.

A new breeze kicked up, a cooler one, out of the west. The sun was getting low on the horizon. I called out to Duke. He raised his head and thumbed back the brim of his hat.

"It's time," I said. "You up for it?"

He nodded and flicked away his smoke and looked at the handful of townsmen standing around him.

"All right, men," he said. "Let's get that cowhand hung."

The townsmen looked at one another. Some went pale.

I asked Duke if he wanted an extra hand.

"You head on yonder," he said. "I got this."

Duke led the men toward the jailhouse.

"Careful," I said. "If I know Cactus Bob, he's gonna kick up a storm, soon as you go pawing at him."

Duke held open the jailhouse door, allowing the other men to step inside ahead of him. He drew his Colt and fell in behind them. The door shut at his back. Seconds later, I heard grunts and punches coming from inside the cell, and Cactus Bob growling in pain through Marshal Pewly's sock.

I turned my back on the jailhouse and crossed the street. The Colts and gun belts had been collected in a leather satchel and placed on the boardwalk between the saloon and Doc Watley's office. I went to retrieve the satchel, then stepped into the office.

Doc Watley and Ms. Twig stood on either side of the bed, Pico lying motionless between them. The boy's skin was ashen. There was only a minimal rise and fall to his chest. I asked Doc Watley if there'd been any change, and he shook his head.

Lily came in behind me and joined us at the bedside. She took Pico's hand. I told her Pico would pull through.

"How do you know?" she asked.

"Got his mother's strong heart," I said.

She looked up slowly. "So you know."

"Yes, Lily. I know it all now."

The doctor turned to me. "I've heard your plan, Searcher."

"And?"

"Do you really expect us to stay in here and tend to this child through all that?"

"We can't get anybody out of town until the cowboys are in," I said. "Stay in here and keep your eyes on the window. When the cowboys ride in, and all hell breaks loose on the street, slip out the back. Join up with the others outside the west end of town."

"The others?" asked Lily.

"The rest of the women."

Her shoulders rolled back. "But I want to fight. All the women do."

"I know y'all do, so forgive how this is gonna sound . . . but this has gotta be a man's fight. We do it right, it ain't gonna be the kind of thing a lady should see. Please know, I say this as a gentleman, certainly not because I don't think y'all capable. Also, the doc'll need you and Ms. Twig to help with Pico."

"And if the cowboys get in here before we can get out?" asked the doctor.

I reached into the satchel and handed the doctor a Colt. "See that they don't."

The doctor slipped the gun into the waist of his pants.

"I don't suppose you can spare another," Lily said.

I looked at her.

"We'll be vulnerable with Pico," she said. "And we won't be able to move quickly."

I reached into the bag for another gun and handed it to her. I asked if she knew how to use it.

"Seen movies," she said.

"That's good enough for me," I said.

She turned the gun over in her hands. "If the moment

comes, I'm not sure I'll be able to pull the trigger. Even if I'm shooting a murderer and a rapist, it goes against everything I stand for."

"I understand," I said. "I hate the very thought of killing, myself. But just maybe there's some men need killin'."

Her fingers went white on the gun handle. "I'm not going to let anyone hurt my child. In the end I guess it's us or them, isn't it?"

"I don't shoot anyone otherwise."

She squeezed my hand. "You're a good man, Sam Searcher."

I tipped my hat, then left the room and stepped into the saloon next door.

Cal was at the piano, mindlessly tapping out notes that didn't seem to be part of any song. The only other person in the room was Tilly, who sat behind the bar, staring off, smoke curling from her cigarette. I walked over.

She poured me a shot of whiskey and pushed the glass forward, keeping her eyes on the bar. I looked at the glass but didn't drink it.

"Something on your mind?" I asked.

She looked up. "I feel like I should have an insult to throw your way. They've always been at the ready whenever you came around."

"Guess I might have deserved a few of them," I said. I met her eyes for a beat, then pushed the drink back, thanked her for it anyway, and started away.

"My soul," she said. "That's what's on my mind."

The piano went quiet.

I turned back. Tilly's eyes had gone wet.

hammers as every Colt in the street swung our way. The horses shifted around anxiously.

"Searcher?" Danyon called.

"Yep."

"You kill my brother?"

"I kept my promise."

"Goddamn you!"

"Figure that's been done already, friend."

Danyon extended his shooting arm.

"I wouldn't pull that trigger." I said.

"Why the fuck not?"

"'Cause I got two men with Marlin Model rifles sighted on your skull, just prayin' that you will."

Danyon scanned the rooftops over both shoulders.

"What happened to my men?"

"I made 'em dead. You're next."

"Fuck you."

I let the silence draw out for a time.

"You know, your brother messed his britches when he stretched," I said, "so I can't rightly say it was a dignified death. You ask me, he's quite the pathetic sight up there."

Danyon shook with rage. He shifted his aim toward the gallows, and his Colt spat a flame. The hanging rope snapped, and the body fell. Danyon set his aim back on me. I was sure he saw me through the slit in the wood. I figured he was about a second away from putting a bullet through that slit.

Speaking to his men, Danyon said, "Get my brother out of the goddamn dirt."

A half-dozen cowboys dismounted and moved to the body.

"Might want to leave the sack on his head, boys," I said. "He ain't quite looking himself since the beating."

Danyon's eyes opened wide, then narrowed again. "Take that goddamn sack off!"

I nodded to Duke and Marshal Pewly.

Duke moved to the back door and positioned himself on the threshold, his Colt fisted at his hip and pointed back into the room. The marshal took a knee where he stood.

I looked outside again and saw three cowboys kneeling on either side of the body in the road. Two of them reached down and removed the noose. Two others pulled the burlap sack off the cowboy's head, only instead of finding Cactus Bob, they found Spittoon Miller, whose shot-up skull happened to be sharing the sack with a coiled rattlesnake named Pam. Pam, I had learned, had not succumbed to Chief's efforts to charm her, so the Indian had resorted to taking her by force, smothering her in his thick denim shirt.

Once free of the sack, Pam uncoiled like a spring. The men kneeling over Spittoon Miller's body leaped back, screaming. Pam landed with fangs bared, her back end chattering. Dust stirred as she slithered into the crowd of cowboys, hissing like a rabid cat.

When her milk-white eyes saw horses, she struck out in every direction. The horses cried and bucked and lurched away. One horse reared, setting off all the others. A few cowboys toppled sideways to the dirt.

A gun fired. I looked down to find a hole smoking in the wood less than an inch from my stomach. I spun clear of the covered window and signaled Marshal Pewly behind me. The marshal pulled the gag from Cactus Bob's mouth.

"Don't shoot!" hollered Cactus Bob. "You'll hit *my* ass!"

Another shot pierced the room with a dusty shard of light.

"Goddamnit, quit shooting!" repeated Cactus Bob.

Seated on the floor, his back propped against the wall, the cowboy looked a mess in Spittoon Miller's blood-drenched clothes. Duke and the townsmen had had to beat him senseless in order to make the switch of clothing. Cactus Bob's face was left swollen beyond recognition. Under the aim of Marshal Pewly's gun, he hadn't made a peep as of yet. Now I was happy to let him speak.

"That you, C.B.?" Danyon called from outside.

"Yeah, Red, it's me!" answered Cactus Bob. "These sumbitches beat my ass to hell."

With a swing of the arm, Danyon ordered some men to rush the jailhouse.

I made it easy for them, pulling the front door into the room and tucking myself behind it. Six men rushed inside. Duke shot the first two. Pewly shot the third.

Behind them, I slammed the door closed and locked it, and the remaining three men turned my way. I shot one of them. Duke and Marshal Pewly rushed the other two from behind, knocking them both unconscious.

Fists pounded the front door from outside.

Cactus Bob squirmed on the floor. He raised his feet to thrust them into Duke's shins, but Duke moved to avoid it, and Cactus Bob connected with the coal-oil lamp instead. The lamp slid across the floor and crashed into the opposite wall. Glass shattered. Oil sprayed. A nearby curtain ignited in flame.

Me, Duke, and the marshal rushed to strip the fallen cowboys of their weapons and gun belts.

The flames grew.

I moved to Cactus Bob, intending to drag him outside, but when I knelt, he drove his head into my chin, knocking me backward.

"That's how he wants it," Duke said. "Leave him."

"We can't," I said.

But Duke took hold of my arm and flung me out the back door. Pewly followed. Duke came out last and slammed the door behind him. We slid a board into a pair of brackets I'd mounted on either side of the jamb, and the door was barricaded.

Duke whistled to signal Chief at the base of the water tower. Me, Duke, and Pewly ran west past the bakeshop to the general store, two doors down. Two townsmen met us at the back door and ushered us inside. We moved straight for the front window.

In the street, some cowboys were still scurrying to settle their horses as Pam continued her rampage. Others had put their focus on the burning jailhouse.

Behind me, Duke distributed guns to the other men, and we all put in fresh loads. I pressed my face to the window. Pegasus and Sorghum stood abreast, facing Chief, thick rope stretched taut between their saddle horns and the tower stilts at their back. Chief led them forward, and the horses jerked their heads and dug their hooves to find purchase in the sand.

my back. I pivoted around and caught only a glimpse of Dan-yon and the six cowboys lined up beside him before they disappeared behind a cloud of gun smoke.

Me, Cal, and Cotton Chatwick answered fire simultaneously.

Three seconds later it was over, and every man who'd fired shots was in the mud.

Beside me, Cotton Chatwick lay facedown, a pool of blood spreading beneath his stomach. On my other side, Calvin was panting in panic, and applying pressure to a hole in his forearm. I felt warmth on my right hip and looked down. Once again, I'd only been grazed.

An eerie stillness had descended over the town. The flutter of fire was the only sound. I kept low. The smoke was slow to clear. In the distance I heard a horse neigh, and then the sound of hoofbeats fading off toward the east.

I peered through the smoky haze and counted six cowboys lying dead in the mud. To the east, the fleeing horseman was already beyond the edge of town. It was Danyon.

"Mr. Searcher!"

Marshal Pewly rushed to my side, out of breath and favoring a shot leg. His face was smeared with soot. A cut above his right eye was caked with sand.

He said nothing, just handed me a gun belt with a loaded six-gun in each holster and helped me to my feet. I tightened the belt at my hips.

There was a snort behind me. Pegasus reared, then came back down softly and stepped to my side. He was lathered and breathing hard. His hide was twitching. I took hold of his saddle horn and swung a leg up. The horse gave no protest.

"I'll come with you," Pewly said.

I shook my head. "Stay here and help with the wounded. Make sure the women are safe."

I didn't even have to spur Pegasus. He was running full tilt by the time we passed the eastern edge of town.

29.

Pegasus closed in quick.

The moon was bright and offered good visibility, and it wasn't long before I was riding through the dust in Danyon's wake. About the time I got a visual on his back, the cowboy started shooting. I bent low over the saddle and shot back. Pegasus held course, pinned his ears, and stretched with every stride.

The southern plateau sloped gradually to the desert floor on its eastern side. Within minutes we'd come to the end of it, where the landscape opened wide and flat.

Pegasus would not be outrun, and Danyon knew it. He suddenly pulled rein and spun his horse around. More shots rang out. Bullets beat the dirt on either side of me. I jerked Pegasus to a halt and returned fire. Danyon spurred his horse again and started back in the direction he'd come, only now he was moving up the plateau.

Soon, he had a clear shot of me from above. He fired off three quick rounds, one of which hit the back of my saddle. I popped the reins, and Pegasus lurched. The horse made the switchback at the base of the slope a minute later, and once again I was in chase at Danyon's back, heading uphill now.

I topped the plateau moments later, and everything seemed to go still. The church loomed some fifty yards ahead. Danyon's horse stood riderless in front of the building.

I tugged Pegasus to a stop and scanned the area as I reloaded both Colts. The dilapidated church had the look of an old Spanish mission. Firelight from the valley below bathed its stucco facade with an orange glow.

I felt vulnerable in the open. There wasn't so much as a shrub around to offer me coverage. I holstered one of the Colts, kept the other one aimed ahead, and heeled Pegasus hard. The horse moved past the front of the building at full speed, then circled around to its west side.

No shots were fired.

I leaped from the saddle while Pegasus was still at a gallop, and rolled when I hit the dirt. The horse continued on, circling around to the back of the church.

I came to my feet below a small arched window. I saw candlelight flickering inside, but the glass was caked with dust, preventing a clear view. I tapped my pistol against the glass, then rolled away, hugging the wall.

There was no response.

Keeping my back pressed to the building, I drew my other Colt and returned to the church's front side. The front door now stood open. I moved toward it, guns extended.

There was laughter from inside, low and taunting.

"What are you waiting for, Searcher? Door's open." There was an echo behind Danyon's voice.

I held my position and my tongue.

"Come on in," he said. "I ain't gonna shoot. If I'd wanted

you dead, you wouldn't have made it within fifty yards of this place."

"I come in there, I'm comin' in blazin'," I said.

"Then I ask again . . . what are you waiting for?"

I tried to swallow but had no spit. My palms had gone clammy. I shut my eyes and steeled myself, then stepped inside the church.

I half expected gunfire, but none came.

Danyon stood at the opposite end of the chapel, some sixty feet up a tiled center aisle. He'd removed his duster. He was heeled with a pistol at his right hip. The other holster was empty. His hands were at his side, extended outward, away from his body. The stub of a cigar burned in the corner of his mouth.

"This what you call coming in blazin'?" he asked.

I didn't respond. I took in the chapel as best I could with peripheral vision. The floor space was clear. Charred and broken pews were pushed against the walls on both sides. Statues, hymnbooks, and Bibles were littered among the rubble, all of them burned.

At Danyon's back was a stained-glass mosaic window, some forty feet high. Much of the glass was broken out. Smoke had blackened the high-vaulted ceiling. The air was dank.

A lit candle stood on its own hardened wax in the center of the aisle, equidistant between us. Danyon's eyes were glassy in the glow of the paltry flame.

Slowly, he raised his arms and clasped his hands behind his head. A smile spread over his face. "Shoot me," he said.

I just looked at him.

"Go ahead," he said. "Sling that Colt."

I wanted to but didn't.

We both stayed quiet for a time.

Danyon's smile grew wider. "That's what I thought." His hands came down, but he kept them extended. "Means more to you to *beat* me than it does just to kill me, don't it?"

"Only thing that matters to me is watching you die, Danyon."

"'Fraid I don't believe that."

"And how's that?"

"Because you hate killin' too much just to shoot me uncontested. That's your weakness, you see."

"You seem to think you have me well figured," I said.

"You wanna quick-draw me, Searcher, because a big part of you is just like me, and you know it. And it ain't enough just to kill that part of you . . . you gotta beat it."

I held his gaze. I knew there was truth in his words.

I asked how much he was heeled with.

"One bullet."

"That the truth?"

"Wanna see?"

"You touch that gun, you die right now," I said.

The cherry of his cigar pulsed.

I flipped open the cylinder of one of my Colts and tipped it. I kicked the bullets away, then tossed the weapon into the rubble at my right. I then removed all but one bullet from the second Colt and set it in the correct chamber to fire. I slid the pistol home at my hip.

Danyon didn't move.

I took a wide stance and loosened my arms at my side. Danyon's right hand began to twitch, just off his holster. My hand was motionless. A breeze hissed in, and the candle flame danced between us for a moment . . . then all was still.

Duke had told me to move first in a gunfight, saying it was a game you couldn't win playing catch-up.

I didn't move first.

I waited for Danyon to jerk . . . and when he did, I caught up.

Two shots were fired.

My bullet hit his stomach.

His bullet hit the ceiling, long after he'd hit the floor.

30.

Alerted by the gunfire, Lily and Marshal Pewly topped the plateau on horseback minutes later, with Chief riding up a few lengths behind.

Tears came to Lily's eyes when she saw me. She came down from her horse and ran to me at the church door. We held a long embrace, saying nothing. Chief and Marshal Pewly remained in the saddle, keeping their distance.

"Pico?" I asked, when we finally parted.

She shook her head. "No change. But he's safe. Everyone's safe."

I glanced at the marshal. With a nod, he confirmed what Lily had said.

Lily's eyes fell to the rifle in my hand. Duke's Winchester. Seconds after Danyon had fallen, it had drawn my eye, its silver stock catching the candlelight where it lay amid all the rubble.

It was unloaded. The barrel had been scratched and dented, and the lever was bent at a curve, as though it had been kicked around. It was clear that Danyon had found the weapon inoperable, and discarded it in frustration.

Lily's eyes came up from the gun.

"It was Duke's," I said. "Don't worry, it's broke."

"Sam, I . . . I heard that he's—"

"He is."

"I'm so sorry." She placed a hand on my shoulder. Then her gaze drifted beyond me, into the church.

"He's dead," I said. "All bled out."

I couldn't tell if her expression was one of relief or disbelief. Probably both. She brushed past me, stepped into the church, and started slowly up the aisle. I fell in behind her and watched as she pulled from her dress pocket the pistol I had given her. She kept the gun at her side.

I stopped midway up the aisle. The clack of Lily's heels echoed through the chapel until she was standing over Danyon's body. He lay prone where he'd fallen, his pallid cheek pressed to the tile in a pool of blood.

Lily's gun hand moved. She set her aim in the center of Danyon's back, and her hand began to tremble.

"It's over, Lily," I said, in little more than a whisper. "You don't have to."

"Yes I do."

There was a series of slow clicks as the gun hammer went back.

I was left with nothing to do but avert my eyes.

And then the dead man rose.

It happened too fast for me to react.

Danyon launched to his knees. Lily screamed. With a lunge, he ripped the pistol from her grasp, turned it on her, and pulled the trigger.

The gun was less than a foot away from Lily's heart when the shot rang out and the barrel spit smoke.

31.

I insisted on bringing Lily down off the plateau personally, atop Pegasus's saddle.

Marshal Pewly and Chief followed on their horses, with Chief leading the two riderless horses by the reins behind him.

Before starting down, we lined up abreast at the cliff's edge and looked down on the town. What few buildings still stood were aflame and soon to collapse. The jailhouse was nothing but charred timber atop a foundation. Only the steel bars of the cell remained standing. The general store was just a flaming skeletal frame. The buildings on the south side of the street were still fully ablaze, including the boardinghouse, the saloon, and Doc Watley's office.

The thirsty earth had already swallowed the water from the fallen tower, leaving the street a quagmire. Saddled horses wallowed and wandered aimlessly. Aided by the firelight, the townspeople were already hard at work. Women trudged barefoot through the mud with their dresses hitched. Men slogged through the street with their pants tucked into their boots. All were sifting through the litter of debris and fallen bodies, separating the things worth salvaging from the things to be discarded.

I was about to cluck Pegasus to move when my ears suddenly attuned to a sound coming out of the south. Running water. I asked Chief what I was hearing.

"Rio Grande," he said, jabbing a thumb over his shoulder. "Lies just behind the plateau, about a quarter mile on. Beyond that's Mexico. Why do you ask?"

"It's not important."

I just nudged Pegasus away from the cliff, and the others fell in behind me.

We were halfway down the plateau's eastern slope when Pewly trotted his horse up beside me.

"Any chance I can get my gun back, Mr. Searcher?"

I glanced over and shook my head. "That gun should stay with Lily."

Pewly's face fell. "But how come?"

"Sentimental reasons, I figure. Just feels like it should stay with her. Anyway, you bein' marshal, I figure it's time you start packin' the real deal."

"Not just caps?"

"Not just caps."

"I reckon not everyone'll go for that, Mr. Searcher, on account I'm not right in the head."

"You proved yourself right capable tonight, Marshal. I don't expect much argument."

"You won't get any from me," said Lily. She tightened her hands around my waist in a knowing squeeze.

"Why thank you, ma'am," said the marshal. Even in the

moonlight I could see him blushing. He tipped his hat, then nudged his horse on ahead.

Of course, I'd known when Danyon shot that Colt at Lily's heart that she wasn't in any danger of taking a bullet.

What I *didn't* know, when I shouldered Duke's Winchester and pulled the trigger a half second after Danyon lurched, was that a bullet was going to come out and find its way into the cowboy's head.

After Danyon had been finished off for good, it had taken Lily some time to regain her composure enough to question what exactly had happened. Some of her questions I was able to answer, but not all.

"It was a toy gun?" she had asked.

"Marshal Pewly's," I said. "Your basic Lone Ranger cap pistol."

"But you gave me that gun yourself."

"I did."

"Knowing that it wasn't real?"

"Yep."

"Because you didn't think I could handle it?"

"Because you didn't want to kill anyone, and I knew it, and I didn't want you to have to. Trust me, it ain't the kind of thing that ever leaves you. I didn't wish that for you. Also, I needed every working gun we had on the street with the townsmen."

"You put me in danger."

"I took a risk. But I knew you wouldn't leave Pico's side, which meant that you also wouldn't leave Doc Watley's side, and I left the doctor heeled with a full load. I knew if the plan went off right that you, Doc, and Ms. Twig would get clear of town with Pico as soon as that tower fell. Which I'm glad to see you did."

"What if the plan *hadn't* gone off right?"

"I can't answer you that. Just glad it did."

With a nod, she indicated the Winchester. "And that?"

"What about it?"

"You told me it was broken."

"It is. I don't figure Danyon would have bent it to hell and tossed it away if it was in working condition. It was also unloaded."

"But it fired for you."

"Fired for Duke, too, when he shot that noose rope at my neck."

Lily folded her arms across her chest. "You had no reason to think that rifle was going to fire and save my life, did you?"

"None."

"So why'd you even think to try?"

"There wasn't time to think. I figure something inside me believed the rifle would fire, and my body moved. Thought played no hand in it."

"But the gun had no bullets."

"It seems to have bullets when it needs to."

"So, what, the gun shoots magic bullets?"

"You said it, not me."

"And how can you explain that?"

"I can't." I raised the rifle and looked at it. "Figure I don't care to, either. It's kinda like trying to explain how I wound up in Blistered Valley, Texas, slinging guns with a long-dead Hollywood legend. It don't seem like it should have happened, but it did. I figure there are some things you just gotta believe in and accept, not study on 'em too hard."

She smiled. "Sam Searcher, I think you got it about right."

The return trip to the valley floor took a half hour. When we reached the town's east entrance, we dismounted and saw what was left of Blistered Valley. It was no longer a town, but a quarter-mile stretch of mud, flanked on both sides by charred destruction. The big blazes had died, and only small, scattered fires remained.

The townsfolk had gathered in a tight group near the well. Their backs were to us, and they were unaware of our presence. Me and Lily exchanged a puzzled glance.

"Searcher!" shouted a voice.

It was Calvin. The old man broke from the crowd and started toward us, calling my name repeatedly.

I jogged out to meet him. Pewly, Chief, and Lily followed.

"We heard a groanin' from down the well, Mr. Searcher!" Cal was breathless and excited. "We sent men down with the chain, and they come up with Mr. Edwards! Alive! There was water in that well! Not much, but enough to save him. He ain't come to yet, but he's sure breathin' good!"

I moved past Cal before he even finished speaking. The crowd parted to make way for me. I found Duke splayed on his back a few feet from the well, the winch chain still draped over his chest and under his arms. His hat was gone. Thick soot and a number of burns blackened his arms and face. His eyes were closed.

Doc Watley was kneeling beside Duke's left shoulder, his ear pressed to the old man's heart. Tilly stood behind the doctor, her hips planted in the mud, her right arm propped against a towns-man's knee for balance. Our eyes met for a beat, and she smiled.

I rushed in next to the doctor, slipped my hand under Duke's head, and raised it out of the mud. I spoke his name in a quiet voice, addressing him as Mr. Edwards.

There was no response. Seconds passed. The crowd was still.

I untied the bandanna at Duke's neck and used it to wipe the sweat from his face. I called out to him again, and this time got a groan in response.

Murmurs passed through the crowd. People shifted around for a better look.

Duke's lips parted, and there came another rumble from his throat.

I said his name again, and he responded again, but I couldn't make out what he'd said. I lowered my ear to his mouth and asked him to repeat. The second time I heard him clear.

"Name's not Edwards," he said. "It's *Wayne*."

32.

We buried twenty-three cowboys and six townsmen the day after the fall of Blistered Valley. Four cowboys remained unaccounted for. Pam, the rattlesnake, was the only woman lost in the fight.

Among the townsmen killed was Mr. Eli Blanton, whose rifle shot from atop the boardinghouse had saved me from a gut shot at close range. I'd insisted on digging his grave personally.

As dawn broke, nails were already being hammered into makeshift shelters, which promised to be the foundation of a new town. The first structure to go up was designated an infirmary. Nothing more than a large lean-to built of scorched plywood, it served to keep the sun off of the wounded, of which there were many. Doc Watley and Ms. Twig worked tirelessly, removing bullets, stitching cuts, splinting bones, and soothing burns. Nearly an entire crate of whiskey, salvaged from the leveled saloon, went to cleaning wounds and sterilizing instruments.

Every task became a group effort. Those who were able lent aid to those who were not. Chief organized a group of men to tend to the horses. Marshal Pewly led another group in gathering discarded guns and unspent ammunition for safekeeping. Tilly served cupfuls of water from the twenty-odd barrels that had survived the fall of the water tower.

Pico's condition remained unchanged. He was alive but unconscious, his pulse still weak, his breathing still labored. When Lily wasn't at the boy's side, she was with me, working alongside the others.

In the first few hours after Duke had whispered his name in my ear, he continued to fall in and out of consciousness. The burn wounds to his arms and face were widespread, but largely superficial. For better or worse, they made him even less recognizable than he'd been before. I figured it yet another miracle that he'd suffered no broken bones in the fall down the well.

Duke didn't come around fully until midmorning. When his eyes blinked open, I was sitting at his side, taking a break from the work, smoking to fight off sleep. He first asked where he was. I told him that could wait, but assured him that he was safe. He asked for a cigarette, and I gave him one.

He remained in a sort of daze after that, only slightly conscious. We talked some, but not much. When we did speak, it was mostly about what was hurting him, which was everything, and what might make it better, which was whiskey and cigarettes.

I knew that his belly pained him even more than the wounds. His hand never left his stomach. At one point, he asked me if I knew why he hurt like he did. I just told him not to worry and said it would pass.

The area buzzed with activity throughout the day. Sleeping

shelters were built. Crosses were hammered into fresh graves. Horses were harnessed and put to work clearing heavy debris.

Around dusk, Duke managed to eat a few soda crackers, but he wasn't able to hold them down.

The whiskey finally, mercifully, put him to sleep just after nightfall.

I drifted off not long after, and the dream came on strong.

I peered upward into the shadow beneath Slick Motley's hat. "Did you lay rough hands on my wife and boy, you son of a bitch?"

He held my stare. "And if I did?"

"I'm gonna make you hurt."

A smile stretched over his face. He reached behind his waist and came around with a knife. The blade gleamed under the porch light as he moved it side to side.

"That's my knife," I said.

"Yes." A laugh rolled in his throat. "And as you know, what once was yours is now mine." The blade went still. "Think hard on what you're about to do, Bonham. You'd be an easy man to make disappear."

"You hurt my family, you bastard. I hope you don't think I'm just gonna walk away."

His knuckles went white on the knife handle. "No, Bonham. You're not."

The knife rose, then slashed downward. I jumped back, feeling the whoosh of the blade pass my shirtfront. The knife immediately came back from the other direction, and I dodged it again. Before Motley could recover, I drove a fist into his

33.

Ahard nudge at the bottom of my boot jarred me awake.

I shot up into a sitting position. I was soaked with sweat. There was a strangling tightness in my throat. I was disoriented in the darkness and yet felt instantly alert.

A shadow passed over my face. Silhouetted above me against the moonlit sky was Duke, fully dressed, his Stetson cocked slightly on his head, the cherry of a cigarette glowing in the corner of his mouth.

"Let's walk."

I stood on stiff limbs, slipped into my boots, and followed him. A cool breeze pushed us toward the western edge of town. We walked without speaking, passing lean-tos under which people tossed and turned in fitful rest.

At the line where the muddy street met the sandy desert, a small hand-built fire burned. The flames were strong. I could see that the fire was fresh. Two bricks had been placed atop the flames, and on the bricks stood a steel kettle. A pair of tin cups sat in the mud nearby. Upturned apple crates had been placed on either side of the fire. We both took a seat, the flames rising between us.

Duke eyed me for some time through the waves of heat. I was still breathing hard, still shaken.

"You were dreaming," he said.

I nodded and drew a heavy breath to steady my heartbeat.

"Man can learn a lot about himself through his dreams," Duke said. "There's truth in 'em."

I nodded again. "There is."

His gaze fell to the fire for a moment, then he looked up again. "I'm dying, aren't I?"

"Yes."

"Stomach cancer?"

"Yes."

"What year is it?"

I told him.

He looked off, like he was letting this settle in, then came back. "How'd I wind up in this place?"

"I found you in the desert, but I wasn't able to bring you out. You tracked me here."

"You know who I am?"

"Didn't when I found you. Do now."

"Who else knows?"

"Only a woman I trust and a boy in a coma."

"No one else?"

I shook my head. "You ain't exactly lookin' yourself. Also, these people have thought you dead for a pretty good spell. They got no reason to suspect otherwise."

"How come that nurse lady to call me Mr. Edwards?"

"That's who you said you were . . . I mean that's who you

thought you were . . . when you woke up. Ethan Edwards. That's the character you played in *The Sear*—"

"I know who Ethan Edwards is."

"Well, anyway, when you popped up out of the silver box . . ." I stopped. "Do you know the box I mean?"

"I'm askin' the questions here." He worked on his cigarette, thinking. "Yeah. I know the box ya mean."

"So you *did* aim to have yourself frozen? Back when you thought you were at your end?"

"I considered it." He looked into the fire. "Didn't go through with it in the end."

"I figure somebody saw to it that you did. Kept it a tight secret, too."

Duke's eyes narrowed, searching his memory. "Tom Mitchell, I reckon. Dr. Tom Mitchell."

"Who's he?"

"Cancer doctor, out in California. Had him some cockeyed ideas about freezin' me till he could cure me."

"You believe any of his ideas?"

"I listened to what he had to say, finally decided he was a quack. Fella seemed crazy."

I considered this. "This Mitchell . . . he a funny-lookin' man with glasses? Got wild gray hair, like Einstein?"

"He wasn't gray in seventy-nine, but yeah. That's him. Where is he?"

"Dead. He was movin' you somewhere in an airplane. The plane crashed, and I found you in that box among the wreckage. Then we both wound up here, and . . ." I looked at him. "Do you remember what all we did here?"

He nodded. "It's been coming back in bits and pieces over the last few hours."

"Well, I guess that's the whole story then." I flicked my cigarette into the fire. "In a manner of speaking, anyway."

"What's that mean?"

"Means there's a few details we haven't covered."

"Why?"

"Long story, I figure."

"We still got a lotta night left."

My eyes fell to the kettle. "That coffee?"

He nodded. Then he pulled a bottle out of his back pocket. I poured the coffee; he added the whiskey. We both lit fresh ones. Then I told him the story.

I told it from beginning to end, starting with my childhood days spent watching him on videotape and finishing with me killing Red Danyon with the Winchester. In between I told him my history, and the history of Blistered Valley as I knew it, leaving nothing out. I even told him about the man I'd killed in self-defense back home, and the wife and son I had to explain it to.

The hours passed slowly, but the cigarettes burned fast. The coffee and whiskey never stopped flowing. Duke took in every word with attentive ears, hardly speaking, his expression rarely changing. Occasionally, he would question a detail, but never the truth or validity of what I was telling him. By the time I finished, the fire was dead. There was light in the east, and people were emerging from the lean-tos on the street.

We turned as the first rays of sun broke the horizon.

Shielding my eyes against the light, my gaze fell on the silhouette of a woman whose shape I'd come to recognize easily from a distance. It was Lily. But it was the silhouette of the young boy standing at her side that pulled my focus. It was an image similar to one from my dreams two nights before. Only now the figures of mother and son didn't fade from my sight, but remained where they stood, waiting for me to join them.

"So tell me, Searcher," Duke said. "Now that you've helped save the people of this town from the bad guys . . . what's next?"

I looked at him. "Figure it's time I rode on. You?"

"Same, I reckon."

We were saddled and packed to leave by late afternoon, and we would have left sooner had Pico not had so many questions about what all he'd missed. Me and Duke answered every one, truthfully and completely, never skirting from the violent acts that had occurred. We felt Pico was man enough to take it, and had more than deserved the right to hear it. His mother made no protest.

Shortly before we left, Marshal Pewly assembled a group of townsmen on horseback. Packed with rations to last a few days, they rode off with the intention of returning with necessary provisions. They'd also sworn to make arrangements to bring in the supplies necessary to begin building a new Blistered Valley in the same mold as the one that had been destroyed.

Before riding out, Marshal Pewly had given me his tin star as a symbol of our friendship.

The remaining townsfolk had gathered at the east side of town to see me and Duke off. We tipped our hats a lot, and hugged a lot of women, and shook a lot of men's hands.

Chief placed his father's turquoise wolf around my neck and told me it would bring me peace.

Doc Watley and I shook hands and shared a nod, and that was all. And it was enough.

Tilly hugged me tight and didn't let go until Cal finally took her in his arms again. When we parted, Tilly asked if I would ever be back. I told her it wasn't likely. She said that she'd never forget me, and I told her the same.

Pico fought back tears as he stepped up to my side.

I mussed the boy's hair. "If it's all right with you, Pico, I'm not going to say good-bye . . . I'd just like to thank you for saving my life. It was a hell of a brave thing you did. And it's something I won't ever forget."

The boy offered his hand, and we shook; when our hands parted, I was holding his harmonica. I mussed his hair again. "You be a good boy to your mama, hear?"

"I will, Mr. Searcher."

Lily stepped up to Duke and kissed his cheek. "You do everything you can to get yourself well," she said. "Promise me."

"Will do, ma'am," he said.

Lily then turned to me. "Your wife and son are lucky to have you in this world, Sam Searcher. I want you to leave here believing that. I also want you to know that whatever debts you owe to man or God have been paid and then some."

"Not yet," I said. "But I'll get there." I hugged her close and held her for some time.

"You're gonna be all right," she said.

"Already am," I said. We parted, and I wiped a tear from her cheek.

With Duke riding Sorghum, and me riding Swift—the same horse that the day before had carried me safely away from the café under heavy fire—we spurred our steeds out of town, heading east at a full gallop, not looking back.

We'd made several miles before Duke suddenly signaled me to pull rein, and we brought our horses to a stop.

"What is it?" I asked.

"I reckon this is where we part ways, friend."

He slipped a cigarette out of his hatband and lit it. His eyes came up slowly. "We both gotta ride on . . . but the way I see it, we're headed down different trails."

"Duke, you're sick as hell!"

"That I am."

"Well, I aim to get you help."

"There's no help for what I got, and we both know it."

"The hell there ain't. We're thirty years moved on from your day. Now'days they got all sorts of—"

"Searcher . . ."

". . . miracle cures and herbal tonics and—"

"*Searcher.*"

"What?"

"I know my fate, same as you. And same as you, I'm at peace with it." He looked off.

"I don't aim to just leave you wanderin' the Texas plain, Duke."

"Well, yer gonna. 'Cause wanderin' the Texas plain is exactly what I want to do with what time I got left."

"That ain't no way for a man like you to die. There ain't nothing out here for you, Duke."

"There's good Texas flatland, which is good enough for me. Now ya gonna keep jawin' on, or shut up and listen?"

I stayed quiet.

Duke folded his arms over his saddle horn. "Ya say ya know my work pretty good, Searcher. So tell me, how'd I always go out in the end?"

I just looked at him.

"With my spurs on, that's how. Not wastin' away in some hospital, wishin' I could smoke." He drew off his cigarette. "Life had given me a lot, Searcher, but you gave me the one thing I'd never had. I spent my whole life playing dress-up. I never had the chance to be a real cowboy till I rode with you. And because of it, I got to go out fighting." He pointed a thumb over his shoulder. "I want you to look back there, tell me what ya see."

I looked back and shrugged.

"Well, I see a sunset I aim to ride off into," he said. "And I reckon it's a good way to go. It's a better way than I had the first time around by a damn sight. I have you to thank for that."

We were quiet for a while, watching our horses twitch to shake flies.

Duke leaned toward me. "You're not gettin' misty on me, are ya, Searcher?"

"Hell no."

"Good. 'Cause a cowboy can cry for his horse or his dog, but nothing else. It don't play well. The audience don't like it."

"Well, I ain't misty." I cleared my throat and sat up straighter in the saddle. "It's just this damn dust."

"That's what I thought." Duke grinned. "Before I shove off, I'd like to ask a favor of ya." He sidled his horse next to mine and pulled his Winchester from the saddle scabbard. "Look after this for me, will ya? But take care with it. I hear it can be a bit unpredictable in the wrong hands."

I took the rifle and set it across my lap. "It shoots magic bullets," I said.

"I know it does."

"Where'd you get this gun, anyway?"

"Only place such a thing could exist." He winked. "Hollywood."

He reined his horse around so that it was facing west, then came back even with me. "Ya know, Searcher, I think I'm in agreement with your lady friend back there. I think you're gonna be all right." He held out his hand and I shook it firm. "Tell your boy I said hello. Make sure he knows our story."

I nodded.

"And don't take nothin' off nobody."

"I won't."

"It's been an honor to ride with you, Mr. Searcher." He tugged his hat brim low, heeled his horse, and moved off.

I didn't turn back. I'd seen the image already, many times over.

I listened as Sorghum's hooves clopped away. When the sound faded off, I reached behind my saddle and tied the Winchester down atop my slicker.

Then I clicked my cheek, and Swift moved off. I kept him at a slow pace, figuring there'd be plenty reason to rush when I hit the next town.

For the moment I was content just to ride, without haste, in the quiet company of a steady horse, a wide-open plain, and the setting sun at my back.

EPILOGUE

FROM THE
WELSHLAND DAILY TELEGRAM

MOTLEY KILLER NOW THOUGHT BY MANY TO BE A HERO

"Sam Bonham might be a killer. But I'm no longer convinced he's a murderer."

This statement was released earlier today by T. S. "Turkey Shoot" Johnson of the Crock County Sheriff's Office in reference to the man for whom Johnson has been searching for more than ten days.

Sam Bonham, 34, is the prime suspect in the slaying of Slick Motley, 35, of Longview. But in a bizarre twist of events, Motley—who was found fatally stabbed outside the residence of Bonham's estranged wife more than a week ago—has since been implicated in the brutal beatings of four women across east and north-central Texas. Officials now speculate that Motley's death may not have been an act of murder, but rather a courageous effort on the part of

Sam Bonham to protect his family. Sam and Georgia Bonham have been separated for six months.

It is not yet known whether Bonham, who remains at large, will face criminal charges in association with the killing, but in the eyes of many local residents, he is already a hero.

"I wouldn't put it past him," stated Elwood Turner, a close acquaintance of Mr. Bonham's. "I know Sam, and if he saw a threat to his family, he'd take action to save 'em. Drunk or not, he got the job done. I'm damn proud to call him my friend."

Other Welshland locals have also come forward to speak on Mr. Bonham's behalf. "Best customer I ever had," claims Edward "Slow Eddie" Mercer, proprietor of a local billiards parlor. "Don't surprise me one bit, Sam riddin' our streets of the bad guy, then clearin' town. That's just Sam's way, taking no credit for his heroism. He'd be welcome at my pool hall anytime."

Some say that the comments of Bonham's estranged wife might best sum up the feeling of an entire town shaken to its core by the knowledge that a ruthless predator might have been in its midst. "He wouldn't have been there for us if he didn't care," Ms. Bonham states. "We owe our lives to him. Now, I just want him to come home."

Printed in the United States
By Bookmasters